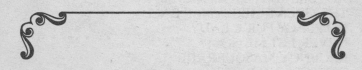

In all their long acquaintance, it was the first time he had embraced her. . . .

He wasn't prepared for the warmth of her response. She went willingly, almost eagerly into his arms, as if she'd been waiting a long time for this. He gazed at her questioningly, and was answered by a silent, provocative shimmer from her dark eyes. Her lips trembled open in an encouraging smile. Without further ado, Luten lowered his head. His lips brushed hers lightly, tentatively, waiting to see how she would react.

At the first touching of their lips, a spark leapt between them and burst into flame. . . .

By Joan Smith
Published by Fawcett Books:

MURDER WILL SPEAK

Joan Smith

FAWCETT CREST • NEW YORK

A Fawcett Crest Book
Published by Ballantine Books
Copyright © 1996 by Joan Smith

http://www.randomhouse.com

Library of Congress Catalog Card Number: 97-90212

ISBN 0-449-22465-1

Manufactured in the United States of America

First Ballantine Books Edition: September 1997

10 9 8 7 6 5 4 3 2 1

Chapter One

The Dowager Countess deCoventry would not, in the normal way, have been caught dead at the Pantheon. This pleasure dome in Oxford Street had fallen sadly from its glory days in the last century, when the nobility vied for admission, to become the haunt of rakes, rattles and lightskirts.

Her escort, Coffen Pattle, said, "If that ain't just like Luten to go throwing his party in a vice den. If it wasn't for Denise, I would not have come. Feel like a dashed man milliner in this sheet, I can tell you."

"Never mind, Coffen. Everyone looks outlandish at a masquerade," the countess replied, as she peered from the window of his carriage at the other masqueraders entering the Pantheon. She counted three lady shepherdesses wearing silken gowns of a sort never seen on the back of a real shepherdess, two gentlemen in the doublet with slashed sleeves, silken hose and duck-billed shoes of Henry VIII, a sprinkling of French court gowns—but no other Cleopatras to compete with herself.

"It was kind of Luten to hold this benefit ball for Denise Leblanc," she said. "How could she support her four children, now that she is too old to dance?"

"She might have thought of that when she had 'em without benefit of a father," Coffen grouched.

"They had a father, Coffen. I think you mean without benefit of a husband."

"Don't be tahrsome, my dear. You know what I mean."

1

"It is you who are tiresome. It takes two to—"

"I know about the birds and the bees. I was just thinking. You don't suppose Luten . . ." He lifted an eyebrow in question.

The countess replied in a voice Beau Brummell had compared to a cello heard in a velvet tunnel, "I shouldn't think so." Coffen, less inclined to hyperbole, thought it was a nice soothing voice. Reminded him of the warble of a thrush. "Denise is a wonderful dancer," the countess continued, "but not pretty."

"A face like a monkey. Pity, for her legs ain't bad."

"Nothing but diamonds of the first water for Luten, you must know. He arranged this benefit ball because he felt sorry for her. He's ashamed of his generosity and is holding the do at the Pantheon to lend it a raffish air."

"Aye, that sounds like him. He wouldn't want to be accused of being softhearted," Coffen replied, satisfied that they had plumbed the little mystery.

It was no mystery why he and the Dowager Lady deCoventry were attending the ball. They were members of the Berkeley Brigade, a collection of young Whig aristocrats who lived on Berkeley Square. They were the acknowledged leaders of the ton, led by the dashing Marquess of Luten. As Beau Brummell had held sway in the previous decade, so Luten was now looked to in matters of style. His horses and carriages, his jackets and coiffures were copied assiduously by his followers, but his real power was in Parliament, where he daily waged unholy war against the King's ministers. Mouldy and Company, the Whigs called them, and fought them tooth and nail for reform.

Pattle's carriage drew to a stop in front of the domed building, they alit and entered the splendid rotunda with its colonnade and glazed dome. The place was done up in the Italian style with frescoed walls and ceilings and a superfluity of statues copied from antiquity. Diffused lighting shone from antique vases hanging on gilded chains from the ceiling and from others atop marble pillars.

They joined the costumed throng moving up the stairway to the painted ballroom. Amidst the babble of excited voices, the haughty accents of Mayfair mingled with Cockney slang and the nasal twang of minor actresses imitating their social superiors. The building, said to hold seventeen hundred, was packed. Lady deCoventry looked around for Luten, who had kept his costume a secret. As his estate, Southcote Abbey, bordered on Sherwood Forest, however, she felt he had probably come as some character from the Robin Hood legend.

When they reached the top of the stairs, Coffen said, "I am going to wet my whistle." As he spoke, his crown of laurel leaves slid over one ear, lending him the abandoned air of a satyr. He was supposed to be Julius Caesar, but had only chosen this disguise as he had forgotten to hire a costume, and a sheet lent itself to the role. There was little of imperial Rome in his actual person. He was short and stout, with a ruddy complexion, blue eyes and mud-colored hair cut in the Brutus do. Even in a toga, the words "John Bull" were written all over him.

"I knew this branch wouldn't stay in place," he said, shifting it back up on his head with an impatient hand. "You had best come with me, Corinne. There's no saying what lowlife coves are hiding behind this collection of masks. I shouldn't be surprised if there ain't a few Tories amongst us."

As he spoke, she espied a tall, broad-shouldered gentleman in a green shirt and matching inexpressibles standing off to the side, surveying the throng. He wore a hat with the brim tilted over one eye and a long feather trailing behind. A quiver full of arrows and a bow were slung over his left shoulder. A black mask covered his upper face. He had one arm placed lightly over a woman's shoulder.

The countess peered to see if she could recognize Luten's companion. She was a statuesque woman with flaming red hair, wearing a black domino. A feathered

3

mask hid her upper face. The countess didn't recognize her at a glance, and she would not satisfy Luten to stare. She knew he had spotted her, because he removed his arm from the woman's shoulder, said something to her and began walking across the room. The countess felt a little thrill of triumph.

"You go ahead, Coffen," she said. "I've spotted Luten."

"Have you, by Jove? What's he wearing?" She pointed to Robin Hood. "Ah, the outfit he wore at his own masquerade party last autumn. Not like Luten to pass up a chance for a new outfit. I leave you in good hands, then."

Coffen went off in search of wine. He had a fair notion that Corinne and Luten were mad for each other. Both too proud to admit it, of course, but one day they would grow tired of snipping and snipping at one another and get shackled. Taking them a dashed long time to get around to it. Corinne's husband had been dead for three years. Some said it was marrying a lady young enough to be his daughter that had put old deCoventry in his grave. She hadn't managed to give him an heir either, which was surely the reason the old gaffer had married her.

Whatever the cause of deCoventry's demise, it had left Corinne in the peculiar position of being the Dowager Countess deCoventry at the tender age of twenty-one years. The earl's heir was his younger brother, already shackled to a lady who was not tardy to establish herself as Lady deCoventry. So here was Corinne, a dowager at twenty-four. Lord, how she hated it. Her friends—all except Luten—had begun by calling her Countess Corinne, now shortened to Corinne. Luten never failed to throw in her face that she was a dowager. Spiteful of him, but that was Luten all over.

Coffen had soon established himself abovestairs in a private box with a bottle of port to pass the time. From this vantage point he looked out on the throng below. The place was so crowded you couldn't swing a flea. Costumes of all colors, dominoes, mostly black, every-

4

one smashed together in a human macédoine. He spotted Cleopatra and Robin Hood waltzing along the edge of the floor.

Corinne's disguise as Cleopatra was well suited to her native endowments. Her whole mien was imperious. For the masquerade, she had followed an illustration found in a book on theatrical costumes. To a plain white gown with a draped skirt she had added a golden border edged in a Greek key design and layered around her neck a quantity of "gold" pinchbeck jewelry set with colored glass. Another of the necklaces she wore on her head, with a gold medallion hanging awkwardly on top of her mask. All of her jewelry was not imitation, however. To add the final note, she had worn, for the last time, the deCoventry pearl necklace. This fabulous item had been brought home from Madras by a deCoventry nabob stationed in India in the last century. It was a long rope of perfectly matched pearls retrieved from the Gulf of Mannar, each one a full fifteen carats. Old deCoventry boasted their lustre was so high they seemed to glow from within, but they looked to Pattle like any other pearls, only bigger.

The necklace was entailed with the estate jewelry, and would soon grace the wattled neck of the current Lady deCoventry. It seemed unfair, when George had paid for it out of his own pocket. His papa had given the pearls to a lightskirt despite their being entailed. George had hunted them down and bought them back for ten thousand pounds, against the advice of his lawyer, who told him he might get a court order and seize them without expense. There was a problem about the statute of limitations, however, and rather than risk losing them, George had paid. He wouldn't have done it if he'd ever thought Corinne would have to give them up. He fair doted on her.

Corinne was unaware of the eyes ogling her as she went to meet Robin Hood. Her crow-black hair was arranged in the Egyptian style with a fringe on her forehead. She didn't intend to wear her mask all evening. Her brilliant green eyes were obscured by the necessary mask, but they might have belonged to an empress. These attributes, her grandmother once told her, had first appeared in the family in the seventeenth century, after some Spanish sailors had found refuge in Ireland from the sinking of the Spanish Armada. The whole family were as proud as Spanish grandees, but unfortunately not nearly so wealthy.

Luten described her as Black Irish, a term she never did quite understand, but felt instinctively was a slur on her origins. She had been raised in genteel poverty on her papa's estate in County Cork. Lord deCoventry was the absentee landlord of a neighboring estate, which he visited from time to time in an effort to jack up his revenues. He had developed a mad passion for Corinne Clare on one of his visits, and bought her from her papa for five thousand pounds. With no better offer in sight, Corinne had accepted her fate. The match had proven relatively successful, despite the disparity in their ages. Corinne was seventeen at the time, one third of her husband's age. He was an undemanding spouse, and she was so charmed with the luxurious life of a London countess that she tolerated any personal inconvenience without complaint. The tears she shed on his death, while not copious, were genuine.

As Robin Hood advanced toward her, she acknowledged his gallant bow with a small smile. Instead of curtseying, she pulled an arrow from his quiver.

"How very like you, Luten. Pointless. There is no head on this arrow." On this jibe, she slid the arrow back in the quiver.

Robin Hood's lips opened in a smile. In the shadowed room, she saw only the flash of white teeth. The orchestra, which had been in brief abeyance, struck up a waltz. Without speaking, Robin Hood drew her into his arms and began dancing. The waltz, while considered racy, was usually performed with a discretion that was lacking on this occasion. Her partner drew her tightly against his chest and began swirling toward a dark alcove at the end of the room.

"This is not a race, Luten," she said sharply. "You nearly capsized that shepherdess and her partner."

When she received no reply, she took a closer look at her partner and wondered whether he was Luten after all. He was the same size and general getup, but something was different. Luten wouldn't hold her this close, for one thing. Unless he had been drinking . . . She discerned a faint aroma of brandy. He waltzed her into the alcove, drew the curtain closed behind them and pulled her into his arms.

She gave a startled leap. "You must be bosky, Luten!" she exclaimed. He didn't say a word, but a gentle, amorous hum from his throat confirmed her suspicion. She felt a trembling excitement and waited to see what he would do next.

One of his hands moved up to brush the nape of her neck, sending shivers along her spine. His fingers felt rough, excitingly so. Then his dark head came down and he kissed her. It was no gentle brushing of the lips, but a real kiss that sent the blood racing in her veins.

The excitement of his brandy-soaked lips provided a strong distraction as his fingers found the clasp of the necklace and unfastened it. The pinchbeck jewelry acted as insulation as his fingers moved so adroitly that she didn't feel the necklace leaving her neck, or realize that Robin Hood had palmed it. The pearls disappeared without a sound into his pocket while his lips nibbled seductively at hers.

Then as suddenly as he had kissed her, he drew back. "Now I must go. Adieu, and many thanks, Cleopatra."

That was when she knew for certain that the man was not Luten. His voice was not a silken drawl, but an uncultured voice. She reached for his hand. "Who are you?" she demanded.

7

A deep chuckle was her only answer as his rough fingers withdrew from hers and he disappeared through the archway, the long feather on his hat bobbing. He was soon swallowed up by the throng of waltzers. She was angry at the fellow's impertinence and embarrassed that she had not only permitted that kiss, but enjoyed it, even if he wasn't Luten.

Chapter Two

Coffen looked to the door of his box as a gentleman in a long, brown, hooded gown entered. The hood was drawn over his head. He lowered his mask and asked in a bored drawl, "Where's the dowager, Coffen? I thought she was coming with you."

It irked Coffen that Luten could manage to look elegant even in a fustian gown drawn in at the waist by a plain cord. The hooded outfit revealed the height and broad shoulders, but concealed his exquisitely barbered head and the dramatic black hair that grew in a widow's peak. A pair of eyebrows as finely drawn as any lady's arched over cool gray eyes with long lashes. It was the strong nose and square jaw that lent a masculine authority to Luten's face. And it was, of course, his thin lips held in a haughty smile that gave it its arrogance.

"You ain't Robin Hood!" Coffen said accusingly.

"No, and you ain't the noblest Roman of them all."

"I never said I was."

"Enough of this persiflage. We were discussing the dashing dowager. What have you done with her?"

"She's with you."

Luten looked all around in mock confusion. "Come as a table, has she? Or a chair, perhaps."

"No, dash it, as Cleopatra. And you're supposed to be Robin Hood. She went chasing after you the minute we got here."

A small smile curved Luten's lips. When he spoke, his bored drawl held a note of satisfaction. "I expect she's

9

discovered her error by now." He would let her seek him out, thus giving him the upper hand.

He eased himself gracefully onto a chair and poured a glass of Pattle's port. He would have preferred claret. Luten had been telling himself for two years that he despised Corinne, yet his instinctive feelings would not be subdued by mere reason. For love of a title and gold, she had sold herself to his elderly cousin. She was an ignorant provincial miss who gave herself airs and cozened society that she was top of the trees. Half of London was in love with her, the masculine half. She paid no heed to his suggestions for her refinement, and even dared to read him lectures! She had hair like spun silk and a complexion that put rose petals to shame. Her eyes made emeralds look dull, and her lips were red and ripe as cherries. What could a man do with such a lady but either hate her or love her? He had offered his love, and she had rejected him. Worse, she had laughed at him.

The humiliation of that entire season was engraved on the marrow of Luten's bones. He had gone to Appleby Court with some thought of offering for his cousin, Susan Enderton. Corinne had been staying with the Endertons that year, after deCoventry's death. Before he had been there a week, he knew it was Corinne he wanted to marry. He suspected he had always known it, and used Susan as an excuse for the visit. He had offered, been refused, and to assuage his pride had offered for Susan, who also rejected him. Half the ladies in London were throwing their bonnets at him, and he had been turned down flat by two provincial misses. He sometimes thought the whole affair had been a nightmare.

Before he finished his glass of wine, Corinne came into the box. "Oh, so that's who you've come as, a monk," she said, lowering her egret mask and tidying her fringe. "Well, it is a masquerade party after all. The sackcloth is up to your usual standard of elegance, but shouldn't there be ashes?"

"Not necessarily. I'm Friar Tuck, Robin Hood's

friend. Coffen told me you went haring after Robin Hood, under the misapprehension that he was myself," he said, with a glint of triumph. He led her to a chair and poured her a glass of wine. She drank it quickly, to calm her nerves.

"I did mean to have a word with you," she allowed, as a hint of rose stained her ivory cheeks.

"I am honored," he said, with a satirical bow. "And what word was that, Lady deCoventry?"

"Why, I meant to congratulate you on the turnout," she invented. "Quite a squeeze. At five guineas a head, Denise can retire in comfort."

"Who was the gent in the Robin Hood suit?" he enquired, and mentally chastized himself for revealing his interest in her partner.

She shrugged. "I don't know. Spencer, perhaps."

"You actually mistook that hedgebird for *me*?" he asked disdainfully. "It is as well known as an old ballad that your eyes are jewels beyond price, but I cannot compliment you on their discernment, Countess. A blind man in a dark room must see the difference."

"I made sure you would come as Robin Hood."

"I was Robin Hood at my own masquerade ball. I don't repeat myself," he drawled. This, whether the countess realized it or not, was a reference to his spurned proposal. "Your regal aspirations, I see, lured you into coming as Cleopatra."

"I don't have regal aspirations, Luten. As you very well know, both the King and the Prince of Wales are married."

"Not all aspirations are realized, or Caro Lamb would be Lady Byron, and Prinney would be slim, instead of a whale."

"And Luten would be Beau Brummell," she riposted.

"Aspirations suggest a desire to better oneself. Luten would be Prime Minister of a Whig government. But you're right; regal was the wrong word. It was imperial aspirations that led Cleo to her downfall."

11

"Don't be pedantic," she said, with a sniff. "May I have another glass of wine, if it is not too much trouble?"

"You put that one away quickly," he said, lifting the bottle to pour her another glass.

"You never miss a chance to find fault, do you, Luten?"

"You provide such a plethora of opportunities, I'm sure I miss half of them."

Their bickering was interrupted by the entrance into the box of another member of the Berkeley Brigade, Sir Reginald Prance, Bart. Sir Reginald was an elegantly slender gentleman with very much the air of a dandy. His main preoccupations were cultural. He painted a little, arranged amateur theatricals, wrote poetry and devoted any spare time to the garnishment of his person. Jackets, cravats, hats, quizzing glasses, snuff boxes and boots were of the keenest interest to the baronet.

Such an opportunity for display as the benefit ball was like manna in the wilderness to Prance. Since Brummell had coerced all the gentlemen to dress like undertakers, he had few opportunities to stun society with his sartorial originality.

For the ball, he had spent hours and a small fortune to rig himself out as a Turkish pasha in satin turban, feathers, yellow harem pants, a long full red coat bedizened with an assortment of jewels and a pair of yellow shagreen slippers turned up at the toes. Stripped of this marvelous array, he was not at all a bad-looking gentleman, although his lean, narrow face always reminded Corinne of a greyhound. He was tall, and possessed of a feline grace.

He performed an accomplished salaam, touching his ringed fingers to his brow, his nose, chin, chest and continuing in a fluid line down to his toes.

"A stunning outfit, Reggie," Corinne said. "Won't you join us? Luten is boring me to flinders."

"Charmed, as always, my dear," Sir Reginald replied,

and lifted her hand to his lips, where her fingers were in some danger of disappearing into his mouth.

He sat down and turned to Luten. "A stunning success, Luten, as we all expected, *ça va sans dire*. I make it ten thousand clear this do will take in. And that without even counting the gallons of cheap wine selling at inordinately high prices." Then he turned his lambent gaze to Lady deCoventry. *"Formidable!"* he exclaimed, giving the word a French accent, and kissing his fingers to his lips.

Coffen narrowed his eyes at Corinne, hitched his slipping crown of laurel leaves back into position and said, "What have you done with it?"

"Done with what?" she asked.

"Your beauty put it quite out of my mind," Sir Reginald said, gazing fatuously. This was a game played solely to annoy Luten. "But surely you were to give the deCoventry pearls a farewell outing this evening, my sweet? So utterly appropriate. Cleo, you know, was fond of pearls. She is said to have ground a pearl into powder and fed it in a glass of wine to Julius Caesar—no, it was Mark Antony. In any case, it had to do with feeding her current *amour* a vastly expensive meal *sans* interrupting the lovemaking by eating."

While he chattered on, Corinne's hand went to her throat. She felt the heavy pinchbeck necklace, but no pearls. Her fingers moved frantically over her breast, thinking the necklace had come loose and fallen into her bodice. "Good God!" She turned to Luten, who was staring in alarm. "I've lost it! It must have fallen off. I must find it at once."

A thundering silence fell on the group as the three gentlemen stared at Lady deCoventry's pearlless throat.

Chapter Three

"Thing to do, we'll go below and look for it," Coffen said. "I know just where you and Robin Hood were dancing. Saw the two of you sliding into that dark alcove."

Luten's delicate eyebrows rose in annoyance. "An odd place to waltz! The alcoves are usually used for more advanced lechery."

"It's gone," she said. The sound of moving chairs overrode her soft words, spoken in a fit of distraction.

The group jostled their way down the thronged staircase to the ballroom, where the waltz was just finishing. Corinne went to the very edge of the room and darted straight to the alcove, with Luten a step behind her. Once inside the little chamber, she remembered those fingers at her throat, and the man's gloating voice as he thanked her. The light from the ballroom was bright enough, and the alcove small enough, that she was soon convinced the pearls were not there. He had stolen more than a kiss.

"He stole them, Luten," she said in a shaken voice.

"Spencer wouldn't do that. Unless for a prank—I'll have a word with him."

Corinne felt a wave of nausea rise up as she considered the ramifications of her loss. She sank onto one of the two chairs in the alcove and sat with her head in her hands, mentally groaning at her predicament. Ten thousand pounds! The court had awarded the pearls to Lord deCoventry. She was to hand them over this coming

Friday. Her lawyer had demanded a period of grace for the countess to consider her legal options. But she didn't plan to get tied up in litigation that might cause a split in the family. They already resented her. Lady deCoventry had used the phrase, "rifled the estate," to describe Corinne's inheritance.

Naturally her husband couldn't leave her anything that was entailed. The family jewels, the country estate and the mansion on Grosvenor Square went to the present lord, but when George saw that no heir was forthcoming, he had used the rents accumulated over the years to buy a house on Berkeley Square and a small country retreat to provide for his widow-to-be. He left her all the monies accrued in his lifetime, amounting to twenty-five thousand pounds. She lived on the interest of it. She couldn't continue living as she now did if she had to give up ten thousand of her capital.

Corinne was not aware of time passing as she sat, brooding over her future. It was ten minutes before Luten returned. His first anger subsided when he saw her so forlorn and worried. He felt a weakening urge to take her in his arms and comfort her. She looked up with hope gleaming in her emerald eyes.

"Did you find Spencer?" she asked eagerly.

"Your Robin Hood wasn't Spencer. He's dressed as Cromwell. He's been with a party abovestairs all evening. Prance went to our box to scan the floor for a Robin Hood. I've been making enquiries. There was only one Robin Hood here. No one knows who he was, and it seems he's left."

The blood ebbed from her face, leaving it white as paper. "He took the pearls with him, Luten. I felt his hands on my neck when he was—when we were—"

"You let him kiss you!"

"I didn't *let* him. He just did it. I thought he was you. I made sure you were drunk," she added hastily. "I didn't want a scene. And as soon as he did it, he thanked me

15

and left. Such a rough, gloating voice. That's when I realized he wasn't you."

Luten found much to dislike in her explanation, and a little something to please him as well. She had willingly gone to the alcove and indulged in an embrace, because she thought Robin Hood was himself. That mention of drunkenness was to cover her embarrassment.

"He's got clean away," he said, damping down the tirade that wanted to come out. "I'll speak to the footmen at the front door. Someone might have seen his carriage, or noticed which way he went. You'd best go back to our box."

"Yes," she said in a dazed voice, but she didn't rise from the chair. He wasn't sure she had heard, or understood.

Luten didn't waste time accompanying her above-stairs. Every minute was important now. He rushed downstairs and spoke to the footmen at the door. They all insisted no man wearing a Robin Hood costume had left.

One of them scratched his head and said, "There was one cove wearing a plain black jacket, tore out of here ten minutes ago. I thought it odd. Most of 'em wore a domino at least, if they didn't want to dress up fancy."

"Did you recognize him?"

"I scarce got a glimpse of him. He had on a mask. He was tall, dark hair. About your own size, milord."

"Did you notice which way he went?"

"I didn't look. I just saw him pelting out the door. He nearly bowled over a couple coming in. I wondered what ailed him, acting so havey-cavey when he was with a lady."

"A lady! Who—"

"She wore a mask as well, and a black domino. A red-head she was, tall, stylish-looking. Not one of our regular bits o' muslin or I'd have recognized her."

Luten stood a moment, thinking. Corinne hadn't mentioned a lady. If they left without Robin Hood's costume, then he must have secreted the outfit in the building. If he had hired it, the costume shop might be able to identify him.

He thanked the man and returned to the alcove, but Corinne had left. He went up to their box, where he found her with Prance and Coffen. She turned her anxious eyes to him when he came in. Again he felt that urge to comfort her. Then he saw that Prance was holding her hand, and he stiffened.

"He got away," he said, and outlined what he had learned from the footman. "Was he with a lady when you first saw him?"

"Yes, a statuesque redhead. I didn't recognize her."

"As she left with him, I assume they came together."

"I noticed her," Coffen added. "I never saw her before, though. Thing to do, have a look around for the duds, eh?"

"But where?" Prance asked.

"I doubt they hired a box," Luten said. "If he came intending to steal a lady's valuables, he'd make himself as inconspicuous as possible. I wager we'll find the green suit in some unused room."

"The gents' necessary?" Coffen suggested.

"There are two. I know where they are," Prance said. "I'll search one, you do the other, Coffen." They left.

"I shouldn't have worn it," Corinne said sadly, rubbing her temples, where a sharp ache was growing. "It was the last chance—I have to return it on Friday. What will I do if I can't find it, Luten?" Panic edged her voice.

"We'll find it," he said, with a conviction he was far from feeling.

"But if we don't—" Her voice stopped on a hiccough of fear. "George paid ten thousand pounds for it. I'll have to give deCoventry ten thousand pounds."

"Do you think he'll make you pay?"

Her face firmed to anger. "His wife will see to that. She's the one who insisted on having the pearls back. She fought over every picture and piece of silver in the house, and Gaviston egged her on. Of course he's the elder son. It will all be his one day. They'll never believe it was stolen. They'll think I hid the necklace to avoid giving it up."

"Let us cross that bridge when we come to it. Meanwhile, we'll leave no stone unturned to find the necklace." That Luten had cropped out in clichés was an indication of his worry. He spoke on, trying to reassure her. "If it was stolen, that suggests the thief is in dire need of money. He'll hawk it, or fence it. We'll be able to pick it up for a fraction of its value."

"I wonder if he robbed anyone else, or just me."

"We'll soon know that, too. If any other lady's jewels are missing, she won't be slow to raise a fuss."

It was Sir Reginald who found the discarded suit, in the gents' necessary room. He came in, smiling in triumph, carrying the suit, hat and quiver and bow.

"He had tossed it in a corner. There's nothing to identify him. The pockets are empty. The footman on duty in the room thinks he remembers Robin Hood going in, but didn't pay him any attention. The man must be eighty if he's a day, and besides, he'd been drinking."

Luten took the costume and examined it. "No label. It's not new, not made especially for the occasion. It shows signs of wear. We'll take it around to the costume shops tomorrow and see if we can discover who hired it."

"He'll have given a false name," Prance said.

Luten lowered his eyebrows and shook his head slightly, indicating that Prance was to adopt a more cheerful tone. "The clerk might have known him. We'll get a description—there might be some distinguishing physical characteristic."

Coffen returned empty-handed. "Oh, I see you found it, Reg. Good. Any clues?"

"Strangely, he didn't leave his calling card," Prance replied.

"Not a complete amateur, then," Coffen said. He was

18

never guilty of sarcasm himself, and didn't look for it in others.

They discussed how they would proceed in the morning.

"In the meanwhile," Luten said, "let's search the building and speak to the manager in case the necklace fell off, and was turned in by some honest soul. You stay with Corinne, Coffen. Prance and I will do the rest."

Corinne gave Luten a small, grateful smile. She noticed that he had called her Corinne, a thing he seldom did.

"Thank you," she said. "Thank you all."

"Don't cry," Coffen said. "I hate to see a woman bawl."

"I'm not crying!"

She gave a sad travesty of a smile, with her bottom lip wobbling uncertainly. It was the image Luten took with him as he performed the chores he had outlined. He felt sure the pearls hadn't fallen off. The mysterious Robin Hood character had them right enough. Who could he be?

His investigations yielded nothing useful. The pearls were not found kicked by accident to the side of the room. No one had turned them in. No other lady had complained of losing her jewelry. Some of the friends he spoke to had noticed Robin Hood. One lady had even noticed him and the redhead entering the Pantheon together, but no one could identify either of them.

When Luten and Prance met up, just before returning to their box, Sir Reginald said, "Do you think the fellow was just after some valuable piece of jewelry he could hawk, or was he after the pearls in particular?"

"Coffen says Corinne went after Robin Hood. I fancy he nabbed the first bit of pricey merchandise he could get his hands on, and shabbed off before it was discovered."

"Pity he chose a Robin Hood costume. That was all that made Corinne think he was you. And by the by, she didn't go after him. He made the first move; she went to meet him. It was pretty well known you wore a Robin Hood suit to your own masquerade ball last autumn."

"I'll bear it in mind, but I expect the fellow just hired the first costume that fit him, and made his play for the first bejeweled lady who gave him the time of day. What would be his point in posing as me?"

"I daresay you're right," Prance said. "We'll have to tell Corinne the bad news. One of us should take her home."

"Someone must stay here and try to discover who was wearing that Robin Hood costume. We'll ask some questions in the street as well. It's not likely, but someone might have noticed which way the fellow went when he left."

"We'll let Coffen take Corinne home," Prance said, with a sharp look.

The matter had been settled between them before they returned to the box.

"Any luck?" Coffen asked at once.

"Not so far," Prance said. "Luten will remain at the Pantheon; I'll make enquiries in the street." He turned to Corinne. "We'll call on you first thing in the morning, my dear. Try not to worry your pretty little head."

"Call on me tonight," Coffen said. "Let me know what happens. I plan to stay up all night, for an hour or so."

Luten took Corinne's hand. "You go home now and try to get some sleep," he ordered.

She looked at him as if he were mad. They both knew how unlikely it was that she would sleep that night.

"I'm sorry I spoiled your party, Luten," she said.

He wafted an elegant hand in dismissal of this detail, then the oddly assorted group went together down to the doorway: Cleopatra, supported on one side by a stout, stumpy Julius Caesar with his laurel branch now slid down over his head to form a rustic necklace; a tall, elegant Friar Tuck on her other side; and a pasha in jeweled turban and harem pants carrying a bundle of green clothing and a bow and quiver bringing up the rear. A few guests recognized the nucleus of the Berkeley Brigade, and wondered what rig they were running.

"If that isn't just like Luten, running away from his own party," Lady Jersey said in vexation to her escort.

Chapter Four

When Lady deCoventry lay in her canopied bed that night, it was not only of the pearls that she thought. She remembered, too, how helpful Luten had been. He even called her Corinne, which was his unconscious way of showing he was in sympathy with her. She was fortunate to have found such good friends in her new home, since her family and old friends were all in Ireland. George had insisted she have friends her own age. She had found it strange that he encouraged her to go about with them, until she discovered it was the fashion amidst the ton for a husband and wife to lead virtually separate lives.

This usually involved having a lover on the side. She didn't think George had had one during their marriage, however, nor had any of her friends ever tried to seduce her, perhaps because she had not yet given her husband an heir. Morals were lax, but gentlemen did seem to agree that a husband had the right to know that his first son, at least, was his own.

It was her cousin, Coffen Pattle, who had drawn her into the Berkeley Brigade. Until George's death, the gentlemen had all behaved like older brothers, protecting her and showing her the ropes. She had missed them more than she missed George during her year's mourning at Appleby Court. They visited once or twice, but it wasn't until the year of mourning was up that Luten had come to Appleby, and made his astonishing proposal.

It had come like a bolt out of the blue. Everyone

22

thought he was dangling after Susan. Corinne couldn't have been more surprised if he'd suggested she run off to Timbuktu with him. And to put the cap on that unfortunate day, she had fallen into a nervous laugh. She was so green she hadn't even realized Luten was the most eligible bachelor in town. She suspected he had offered out of pity, and she had refused without a moment's hesitation. Even if he had meant it, she would have refused. She had made her debut into society as a married lady at seventeen years of age and never enjoyed that special season as a girl to be courted. She had wanted that.

After a few months, though, she went back to her old friends. The only difference was that Luten had taken her in dislike. Pride forbade her from indicating to a snide, cynical Luten that she had changed her mind. He never gave her the chance—until tonight, when she caught a glimmer of the old Luten. They would all stick by her during this ordeal. It was on this warm thought that her eyelids fluttered closed, and she slept.

She used to lie in bed in the morning, gazing at her beautiful chamber, thanking her lucky stars that she was not back in Ireland, sleeping with her sister Kate in that drafty room with the faded curtains and pink, distempered walls. This room was not so grand as her bedchamber at deCoventry House, but it was equally beautiful. She had chosen most of the furnishings herself after George's death. The few pieces she had been allowed to take from George's house were in other rooms. For this, her own bedchamber, she had chosen delicate white French pieces trimmed in gilt, with apple green lutestring hangings for her bed and windows. They glowed in the sunlight, emitting a golden sheen, but on the morning after the masquerade, she paid her room no heed.

The first thing she saw when Mrs. Ballard drew her curtains was the Cleopatra gown hanging on the door of the clothespress, and it all came rushing back to darken

23

her day. The clock on her toilet table told her it was eight-thirty.

"How was the masquerade ball?" Mrs. Ballard asked brightly. "You were home earlier than I expected."

"It was horrid! Has anyone called, Mrs. Ballard?" she asked, picking up her cup of cocoa.

Corinne had been frightened of deCoventry's servants when she first married. George had found her a positive mouse of a lady, the widow of a distant clergyman cousin of his, to be her companion-cum-dresser and personal maid. Over the years, Mrs. Ballard had become a friend and acted as chaperone when one was required. When a widow was so young and so dashing and had gentlemen running tame at her house, it was well to make this nod to propriety. Although Mrs. Ballard was officially her companion, she refused to give up her former duties. Corinne usually told her friend all her secrets, but she didn't plan to share this one, lest word got back to deCoventry. Her hope was to find the pearls and never admit she had lost them.

"Lord Luten called half an hour ago. He said not to awaken you, milady. He left a note." Mrs. Ballard nodded to the tray, where a folded note was stuck beneath the cocoa pot.

"Thank you. I expect I shall be going out this morning. I'll wear my violet walking dress."

Corinne read the note while Mrs. Ballard scuttled about, tidying curtains and arranging her toilette. The note, written in Luten's bold scrawl, was brief and to the point:

Dear Corinne,

We had no luck last night but plan to begin touring the costume shops, jewelry shops and fences as soon as they're open for business. Send word as soon as you are up and about.

Sincerely, L.

She finished her cocoa, hopped out of bed and darted to her desk, where she scribbled off an even briefer reply, with the new patent pen Sir Reggie had given her.

Dearest Luten,

I am up. Please come at once! And thank you, with all my heart.

Corinne.

She sat a moment, wondering if the "Dearest" was a shade warmer than it should be. No, he deserved it. She gave Mrs. Ballard the note. "Send this to Luten at once, please."

Luten's house was directly across the street from her own. While she was dressing, she saw Little Jack, the footboy, run across the street with her note. He wore the deCoventry livery of moss green with gold lace, the green chosen to denote deCoventry's connection with Ireland.

When she was dressed, she went to the breakfast parlor but didn't remove the lids from the hot dishes on the sideboard. The very aroma of bacon made her feel nauseated. She just had a cup of coffee and waited for Luten to come. In her eagerness, she took her cup to the window that gave on Berkeley Square. On either side of the broad flagstoned pavement were protective wrought-iron railings. The houses were all similar, made of either gray or brown brick, though varied as to size. The façade of Luten's large mansion was unadorned save for the pedimented doorway, flanked by white pillars, and reached by stone steps with a lamppost at the top. On the oak door a brass lion's head knocker as big as a saucer gleamed in the sunlight.

As she watched, Sir Reginald Prance, with his shirt collars riding above his jacket, came gliding down the street and turned in at Luten's house. He lived two doors up the street. Not much later, a much less elegant Coffen Pattle, whose home was next door to Corinne's, was seen ambling across the street to Luten's. A rush of gratitude warmed Corinne's heart to know they were all meeting to help her. Within a minute, Luten's door opened and the three gentlemen, looking like badly matched triplets in their curled beavers, blue jackets, fawn trousers and shining topboots, came out. She felt a sense of security, of confidence amounting almost to pride, to see them striding purposefully, side by side, to her rescue. The solidarity of the Berkeley Brigade was legendary. If you offended one, you offended all, and the consequences could be dire. Doors to the best clubs slammed, invitations ceased to arrive, credit could be cut off.

The three gentlemen crossed the street to disappear from view as they mounted the stairs to her front door. She was in the hall to greet them. Her eyes flew to Luten, who was gazing at her with an unreadable expression. He smiled, trying to reassure her, and she smiled back in acknowledgment of his effort, but there was no real joy in either smile.

Black, her butler, regarded them all with the keenest curiosity but was too well trained to ask any questions. He would learn soon enough. Black was an accomplished eavesdropper. He could hear a feather fall on a down pillow. He had the sharpest ear and the softest tread in London.

She led them to the Green Saloon, an elegant chamber done in the Adam style, with two matching fireplaces and classical decoration. The room was too small for the massive, gilt-laden furnishings to be seen in most noble mansions, but the light, feminine decor pleased Corinne. As soon as greetings were exchanged, Luten spoke.

"We decided that Reg would go after the known fences and Coffen will take the Robin Hood outfit to the costume shops. I'll visit the jewelry shops. The pearls won't likely be in circulation yet, but we'll ask the shopkeepers to notify us at once if they turn up. I expect you'd rather join one of us than sit worrying. Of course it will be ineligible for you to accompany Prance. He'll be venturing beyond the precincts of the polite world. If you'd like to come with either Coffen or myself . . ." He finished with an air of indifference.

"Yes, I'd like to go with you," she said to Luten.

"Do you have a description of the pearls?" he asked, not making a display of his little triumph, but obviously happy with it.

"There are one hundred pearls in the necklace, each close to one half inch in diameter. It's so long I usually wear it knotted. The clasp is shaped like a laurel leaf, picked out in diamond chips. The pearls are strung on a braided cord of fine gold wires. The lustre is supposed to be something special. They're unique; there's no possibility of their being mistaken for any other pearls."

"One thing I omitted to ask last night," Luten said. "Are they insured?"

The three gentlemen waited with bated breath. As she shook her head, their hearts sank. "No. The insurance premiums have become so high with all the robberies that I don't insure my jewelry." Such little economies were common.

"That was demmed foolish of you!" Luten said grimly.

"Too cruel, Luten!" Prance exclaimed, putting a protective arm around Corinne's shoulder. "The fault is mine. If you must roar like a lion and lash your tail, do it to me. I advised Corinne to skimp on the boring necessities and indulge herself in the luxuries."

"You would! The blind leading the blind."

"Don't be tahrsome, Luten," Coffen said. "No point crying over spilt milk after the horse has bolted."

"Damme, I shall insure my bits and pieces this very day," Prance declared. "The price is stiff, but worth it. If I should lose my diamond cravat pin . . ."

"Well, are we off?" Coffen said, rising.

The others rose as well. "Where shall we meet up, and when?" Prance asked.

27

"I want you all to come here for luncheon," Corinne said. This was agreed on.

Coffen gave Corinne's shoulder a crippling squeeze. "Cheer up, Corrie. It's always darkest at night."

On this pithy encouragement, he took Prance's elbow and led him out. Corinne went to speak to Mrs. Ballard about the meal, and to put on her bonnet. When she and Luten went out, his shining yellow curricle with silver appointments, drawn by a team of matched grays, was waiting at the roadside. His tiger was a freckle-faced lad. He had once been stuck in Luten's chimney for fourteen hours while sweeping it, and had been rewarded by being allowed to remain at Southcote Abbey in the beginner's position of backhouse boy. He had displayed such a knack for horses that he soon reached the eminence of tiger in charge of his lordship's curricle and team. He wore a disappointed face as he vacated the driver's seat and tossed the whip to Luten. The sporting carriage held only two passengers.

"Cheer up, Scamp," Luten said to him. "I have to drive 'em myself from time to time, to keep up my skill. You can ride bobbin in the rear. I'll need you later."

Scamp's ruddy face was wreathed in smiles as he hopped onto the back of the rig. They were soon bowling along Piccadilly toward New Bond Street. Already the streets were alive. A crier with cocked hat and flaxen wig was ringing his bell to announce the public execution of four highwaymen that afternoon. Postmen in red and gold went about their business. Somewhere, a church bell was pealing.

They alit to begin visiting the jewelry shops, while Scamp had the pleasure of taking the reins. They began with the bigger and better known shops: Rundell and Bridges, Love and Wirgams. When they had no success there, they sought out the less-known purveyors of jewelry. The story was the same everywhere. No one had seen the pearls.

Luten tried to keep Corinne's spirits up as they kept

meeting a blank wall. "Very likely Prance will have learned something," he said on one occasion. And on another, "Perhaps Coffen's had some luck with the costume."

"We're bound to discover something," she said. "They couldn't just disappear into thin air."

Luten left a card with each proprietor, with instructions to notify him immediately if the pearls showed up. He also gave a description of the man who had stolen them, although this was not necessarily the same man who would try to sell them. At Corinne's suggestion, he also gave the description of the redheaded woman.

"The necklace is stolen," he explained. "Tie up the scoundrel who has it and call Bow Street. There's a reward in it for you."

"How much?"

Luten looked to Corinne. "A hundred pounds," she said.

"Make that two hundred—and our undying gratitude," Luten added, to give them the notion there would be increased business in future as well.

"I never realized there were so many jewelry shops in town," Corinne said, after they had visited a dozen. "And this is only London. If they've been spirited out of town . . ."

"It's not likely a provincial would have heard of our masquerade. It's a London cove who took them." He didn't add that a really sharp prigger might very well take stolen goods out of town, or out of the country to sell. "At least it wasn't diamonds," he continued. "A set of diamonds might be broken up and the stones sold separately, but pearls drilled through for a necklace aren't much good for anything else. Their value is in their being well matched."

"That's true," she said.

"Our morning was unfruitful, but it had to be done," Luten said, as they drove back to Berkeley Square. "We may hear back from one of the shops in a day or two."

"The pearls have to be handed over by Friday," she reminded him.

"That leaves us four days. Plenty of time," he said confidently. "And we still have to hear from Reg and Coffen."

When he drew to a stop in front of her house, she reached out and took his hand. "I want to thank you, Luten. Even if we don't find them, I have found out what good friends I have."

Her throaty voice always acted like an aphrodisiac on Luten, but on this occasion, his main response was pity. It was unlike Corinne to be so gentle with him, almost self-abasing. He disliked it and said gruffly, "I'm sorry it took a crisis to make you realize it."

He heard an echo of her old cockiness when she replied, "There's no need to turn a compliment into an insult. Have you so little experience with praise that you can't respond to it in a civil manner?"

"I have no experience of receiving praise from *you*."

"What have you ever done to merit praise—" She came to an embarrassed pause. "Until now," she added sheepishly.

"What can one do for a lady who has everything? A home of her own, an adequate income, friends past counting, more suitors than she knows what to do with."

Was that how Luten saw her? As a lady so independent she didn't need him? "One can never have too many friends. And my income is hardly adequate."

"It seems sufficient to keep you turned out in the first style of fashion. A pity you hadn't bought insurance, instead of that gaudy new Tilsbury."

"I needed a carriage. You know deCoventry took all George's."

They went bickering into the house, to be met by an excited butler. Corinne knew at a glance that Black had been up to his old eavesdropping tricks. A smile creased his saturnine face and his black eyes gleamed.

"Mr. Pattle has returned, milady. He is wearing a hole in the carpet in the saloon. We'll get them back, never you fear."

"Thank you Black," she said dampingly, just before darting into the saloon to learn what Coffen had discovered.

Chapter Five

Coffen paced to and fro in front of a striped satin sofa, carrying the Robin Hood costume in his arms, with the bow and quiver wrapped up inside it like a baby in a blanket.

"I came as soon as I heard. You'll want to be along for the quizzing. You will know what to ask," he said. When his listeners blinked in confusion, he realized he had not delivered the cream of his story.

"Did you find out who hired the suit?" Corinne asked, in considerable excitement.

"I didn't, but I learned it wasn't hired from a costumer." This deflating news hardly accounted for his proud pacing, and his talk of "quizzing." He continued, "Tess Burnbridge, the costumer in the Strand—you remember her place, Corinne, where we went for Luten's masquerade party. His first one—"

"Yes, yes. I remember."

"Tess says this suit comes from Drury Lane Theater. She explained how she knew. Something to do with the cloth and the cut. They pad out the shoulders and nip in the waist to give a figure onstage. She spotted grease paint around the collar, there where you said it was worn, Luten. It ain't dirt; it's grease paint. We're looking for an actor down on his luck."

Corinne listened, frowning. "He didn't speak like an actor. His voice was uncultured."

"There you are, then. He was acting as if he wasn't an actor," Coffen told her.

"Is this luminous stupidity, or does he have a point?" Luten murmured.

"There must be some link to Drury Lane," she said. "We shall go there this afternoon. Thank you, Coffen. Our own morning was futile. We learned nothing. I wonder how Reggie fared."

Even as she spoke, Prance was approaching the house. He was soon shown in by Black. Sir Reginald tossed up his white hands in a gesture of defeat. "Nothing. *Nada. Absolument rien.* I have spent a degrading morning rubbing shoulders with the canting crew, all to no avail. I expect I smell of kippers. I shouldn't be surprised if I've contracted lice. I swear—"

"Don't make a whole soliloquy out of it," Coffen said.

"You mistake the nature of a soliloquy. It implies talking to oneself, but I am encouraged that you know the word, Pattle. To summarize briefly—"

Coffen drew a deep breath. "If this is brief, I'd hate to hear long."

"No one has seen the pearls," Prance said. "I put out word to contact us if they turn up. A certain cove by the name Dirty Dick, in honor of his hands one assumes, or perhaps his jacket, was recommended to me by a racetrack tout I know. Dirty Dick, it seems, will intuit when the pearls hit the street. He is a clearinghouse of purloined goods, a one-man Stop Hole Abbey. My butler will disown me if Dick comes to the front door. Any luck here?" On this speech, he lifted his coattails and sat down.

Coffen repeated his story. "It hardly solves the case, but it's better than nothing," Prance allowed grudgingly.

"It's a start," Coffen said. "Rome wasn't burnt in a day."

"No," Prance said. "It took nine days, if one is to believe Suetonius."

"What the deuce are you talking about?" Coffen demanded.

"The burning of Rome. Nero, the fiddle. You've heard of Nero."

"Nero Forini, the cobbler on Old Bond Street? I never heard he was an arsonist!"

"Actually I was speaking of Nero Claudius Caesar, the well-known fiddler. Obviously you don't have the gentleman's acquaintance, despite your three months at Cambridge, but you have done well in finding where the costume comes from, Pattle."

It lent a ray of hope to their luncheon. Corinne informed Mrs. Ballard what was afoot as soon as they sat down at the table. There was no hope of Coffen keeping his tongue between his teeth. Mrs. Ballard flew into a twitter and said she would pray for the recovery of the pearls.

"Then the matter is solved," Prance said, rolling his eyes in disparagement. Corinne kicked his ankle under the table.

"Forgive me, my pet," he murmured, "but you know I was always prejudiced in favor of common sense."

"Never guess it to listen to you," Coffen muttered.

Luten, watching this performance, felt a pronounced desire to box Prance's ears. To garner Corinne's attention, he said he had heard the results of his masquerade party that morning before leaving home. The charity ball had netted twelve thousand pounds for Denise. The sale of wine had helped.

"If all else fails, you can have a charity ball for Corinne, to recoup the price of the pearls," Prance suggested.

"I'm not a charity case!" she exclaimed. "I could always sell my country retreat."

"Never sell land if you can possibly avoid it," Luten said. "Sell jewelry, if you must. Don't sell your real estate."

"And wear paste stones?" she said with a sniff.

"My dear, who would bother to glance at mere diamonds and rubies when he might feast himself on your emerald eyes?" Prance said, with a sly grin toward Luten.

"Thing to do," Coffen said, "find yourself a rich husband, Corinne. You won't have any trouble."

Corinne had been sold once. She had no intention of repeating the process. She kept her eyes averted from Luten, who gave Coffen a scalding look over his wine glass.

"Is the wine off?" Prance asked him mischievously. "You look as if you were sipping vinegar, Luten." Luten glared. "I cannot agree with Pattle myself. What Corinne must do is take a lover. A lover is more likely to shower you with diamonds than a husband, *ma chérie*."

Mrs. Ballard gasped; Luten glared again.

"No need to put on your crown of thorns, Luten. I was only funning." Prance pouted.

Luten ignored him and said, "We don't want to incite too much curiosity by all of us going to Drury Lane this afternoon. Who will undertake the job?"

"No reason we need incite curiosity," said Prance, who liked nothing better. "We shall claim we're looking for an actress who can sing a few songs in an amateur theatrical we are putting on. I've done it before. You remember my version of John Gay's *Beggar's Opera*, Luten? I was Peachum; you Macheath, the highwayman. A masterstroke of casting."

"And I got stuck playing the warder of Newgate," Coffen said, picking up a stalk of asparagus.

"I wish you would use a knife and fork." Prance tsk'd, shaking his head. Prance's aversion to touching his food with his fingers was well known. He was the only man in London who ate olives with a knife and fork.

"When Rich produced it for Gay, it was a vast success," he reminded them. "It was said the play made Gay rich, and Rich gay. Mine was less successful. It made Prance stumble, financially speaking. Caro Lamb made a disastrous Lucy. Who was that actress we hired to play Polly, Luten? We might have a word with her."

"She's left the theater," Coffen said. "Albany took her under his wing. I see her trotting about town in a phaeton pulled by a pair of matched cream ponies."

Mrs. Ballard did not gasp this time, but she cleared her throat to remind them there were ladies present.

"We can hire costumes, since that's what we're interested in," Luten said.

"Everyone knows I would design the costumes myself," Reg objected at once.

"We're not really putting on a play, Reg," Corinne said.

Prance, wallowing in deepest sulks, announced that if Luten planned to take over, he would change into his oldest jacket and continue quizzing the fences. He left in a huff immediately after lunch. Coffen, who adored actresses, opted to go to the theater with Luten and Corinne.

As they were three, they took Coffen's closed carriage. Drury Lane, recently rebuilt after burning to the ground, was a magnificent mixture of marble and porphyry on the outside, changing to faux porphyry and faux classicism within. Plaster statues and plush sofas decorated the long foyer. A rehearsal was in progress on the stage, where a weary director said, "Try it again, dear, and with feeling this time."

They worked their way around to the back of the theater. Coffen, an habitué of the three Green Rooms, was familiar with the route. Even in the afternoon, there were actresses and their hopeful patrons in the Green Room to which Coffen led them. The girls were eager to escape the cramped rooms they called home. Wine was being served, along with plentiful flirtation.

Coffen approached a plump and saucy redhead. "G'day, Amy."

She dropped an exaggerated curtsey. "Mr. Pattle. Always happy to welcome you, I'm sure."

"I am here on business," he said sternly. "We want to hire costumes for a play we're putting on. Who would we see?"

"Mr. Brown. You'll find him down the hall two doors."

"Thankee kindly."

She placed her hands on his lapels and looked at him archly. "Will we see you tonight, Mr. Pattle?" she asked.

He turned slightly pink around the ears. "I shouldn't think so," he replied, and fled the room. He preferred to do his flirting without Luten's steely gaze on him.

They proceeded down the hall and tapped on a plain door painted dull gray, and bearing Brown's nameplate.

"He is sporting his oak," Coffen said. "I hope he ain't with a lightskirt."

At once a voice called, "Come in."

Mr. Brown was alone, seated at a table littered with sketches and swatches of materials. He was a poor man's version of Sir Reginald Prance, a tall dandy with a lean face.

"Come in, come in," he said. "Ah, Mr. Pattle. This is not your usual port of call at Drury Lane. How can I help you?"

Coffen gave the story about wanting to hire costumes.

"I'm up to my ears in costumes," Brown said, gesturing to the confusion on his table. "One is hard put to compete when Covent Garden has been turned into a circus with live elephants and horses."

"*Bluebeard,*" Coffen nodded. "A dandy show."

"We're countering with a Turkish extravaganza featuring a dozen harem girls. Byron has created a taste for such exotica. What sort of costumes are you after?"

Coffen looked to Luten. "We're doing a dramatic version of Robin Hood," Luten said.

"You just might be in luck. All our costumes were lost in the fire two years ago, but we mounted a modest comedy last year based on Robin Hood. It didn't take, closed in a fortnight. Rose Grimm looks after the costumes. You'll find her belowstairs. As you contributed so handsomely to the building fund, Mr. Pattle, there'll be no charge."

They thanked Mr. Brown and left. The decor belowstairs lacked the sybaritic marble and plush of the lobby. There was no carpet underfoot as they continued down a winding staircase to what could only be called a cellar. The bleakly cavernous room was dimly lit by dusty half windows near the ceiling and rush lights on the wall. They found a pale, pretty blond girl seated at a table with another girl, repairing used costumes. They were both huddled in shawls against the clammy, subterranean air.

"Which of you would be Rosie Grimm?" Coffen asked.

The blonde looked up, frightened. "I'm Rosie Grimm, sir."

He repeated his story. "It's all right. Mr. Brown told us to see you," he said, to allay her fears.

"Them costumes were burnt up," Rosie said. "In the big fire, you know."

"No, they wasn't, Rose," the other girl said. She was more robust than Rose, with dark curls, but less pretty. "That play was only put on last year. I know just where the costumes are. Come along, gents. They're this way."

She led them to the rear of the room, where aisles of costumes hung on hangers, covered with muslin to protect them from dust and the smoke of the rush lights. The rows were marked with the name of the play the costumes had served.

"Here we are," she said, gesturing to a rack of costumes, many of which were green suits. "These were worn by the chorus of merry men," she said, "and here is Maid Marian's dress. Ever so nice, innit? Annie looked a sight in this blue gown, with a dandy white mantle over it."

Corinne noticed one hanger holding only a muslin cover. "May we see Robin Hood's costume?" she asked.

The girl, her name was Phoebe, began rooting through the hangers. "Now that's odd! It should be here, but I can't find it. I'll ask Rose." They followed her back to the sewing table, where Rose sat, tense and listening.

"The Robin Hood suit is gone," Phoebe said. "Did somebody take it out, Rose? You mind some of the girls wanted costumes for that swell's masquerade at the Pantheon last night."

"They brought their gowns back this morning," Rose said. "They borrowed the French court gowns and wigs. Nobody used the Robin Hood suit." As she spoke, she cast a few timid looks at the callers. Corinne noticed she had pierced herself with the needle. A small droplet of blood grew on her thumb.

"Maybe somebody took it without leave," Phoebe suggested.

"No! I locked the door when I left. No one took it," Rose insisted. "Don't go telling Mr. Brown it's gone, Phoebe. It's more than our jobs are worth. You mind he turned Hilda Pigeon off for borrowing the lace off that Lydia Languish gown."

Phoebe shrugged her shoulders. "Sorry, sir. The Robin Hood suit is gone. Do you want to hire the rest of them?"

Luten smiled in a kindly way. "I'll think about it. Our little drama doesn't actually feature the merry men. It's a small production. It's not likely the Robin Hood suit would have fit in any case. What size was it?"

Rose's tongue flicked out and moistened her lips. It was Phoebe who replied. "It was about your size, sir, wouldn't you say, Rose?"

"Smaller, I think," Rosie said. "Yes, certainly smaller."

"It never was!" Phoebe said. "You mind Charlie Molton wore it. He's well built, like this gentleman." She tossed a bold smile in Luten's direction.

"A little shorter," Rose insisted. Naked fear gleamed in her eyes.

"Well, thank you very much for your trouble, girls," Luten said, and placed a gold coin on the table.

Once outside the door, the three exchanged a sapient look.

"Rose knows more than she's telling," Luten said.

Coffen said, "She was scared as a rabbit. Daresay she was put off by so many of us. If you got her alone and had a go at her, Corinne, she might open her budget to you. One woman to another, so to speak."

"Yes," Corinne said. "It would be better to do it away from the theater. I'll ask her where she lives."

"Don't ask her; it will only put her on her guard. The manager would have a list of employees," Luten suggested. He turned to Coffen. "You're in high aroma hereabouts, Coffen. You ask the manager. Feign a romantic interest in Rose Grimm."

Coffen looked deeply offended. "I don't go out with seamstresses! I'll tell Wilson I want Rose to make us up some costumes in her free time."

Luten and Corinne waited for him in the lobby on one of the plush sofas. While they sat, discussing Rose's fear and its probable cause, Phoebe came running through the lobby. She made directly for them.

"I don't want to be a snitch, but I might be able to help you. A girl in my position, trying to keep out of the poorhouse on the pittance they pay us here," she added, with a meaningful glance.

Luten drew out a coin and she snatched it. "Rose took a costume home last night. She swears black is white it was only a ripped hem from one of the costumes she was repairing. No such a thing. Why would she wait till night, and take it home with her? She's been nervous as a tick all day. I figure she borrowed it for her fellow, meaning to bring it back before it was noticed. She's no thief, is Rosie."

"Do you happen to know her fellow?" Corinne asked, forcing her voice to calmness.

"You'd think he was an archbishop the way she makes such a secret of him, but she's got someone on the string lately. I've never laid an eye on him myself. She says he's a gentry cove. Married, I wager, or why does she keep mum about him? There's another fellow after her, there where she lives, on Stukeley Street. Why would she bother with the likes of him for? He's only the caretaker

40

of the block of flats. He don't own it. Oh there's plenty of lads would be happy to set Rose up."

"A block of flats on Stukeley Street?" Luten asked.

Phoebe drew a deep sigh. "Not really flats. A rooming house. That's all the likes of us can afford. It's hard . . ."

Luten handed her another coin. "The big gray brick place just off Drury Lane, below High Holborn. The second house from the corner. You can't miss it. You won't tell her I told you!"

"No. What time would she be home?" Corinne asked.

"It being so close, like, she nips home for a bite between five and six. We have to be back by six-thirty, in case we're needed to do any little repair work before the play starts."

"Thank you, Phoebe," Corinne said.

Phoebe looked all around before darting off. It was another ten minutes before Coffen joined them.

"Wilson's not in his office. I had a look about, but—"

"It's all right. We got Rose's address," Corinne told him.

"Eh? How did you manage that?"

They told him about Phoebe's visit.

"I'll call on Rose at home later," Corinne said.

"You shouldn't go to a place like that alone," Coffen cautioned. He looked to Luten. "We'll wait outside in the carriage?"

"I would appreciate some company," Corinne said, "but I'm sure you two have things you should be doing."

"I have to meet with a banker and set up a trust for Denise this afternoon," Luten mentioned. "I shall call for you around five. No need for us both to go," he added to Coffen.

"I'll let you handle it, then. I must be stepping. I am promised to my aunt for tea. She's trying to match me up with a cleric's daughter. I'll take the chit for a hurl in my rig, but I'll be dashed if I'll marry her."

He left them at Berkeley Square, where Luten accompanied Corinne to her door. Seeing her anxiety, he wanted to comfort her. "It's only a necklace, Corinne, not the end of the world."

She was in no mood to have her troubles belittled. "I didn't really expect you to understand," she said stiffly.

His voice, when he replied, was as cold as steel. "I lack Prance's ingenuity in suggesting ways out of the situation, but whatever I can do to help, you have only to ask."

"Thank you, Luten." She left before he could say more.

When Corinne entered the house, Black met her. "Lord Harold is waiting for you in the Green Saloon, milady."

Lord Harold Eden was deCoventry's younger son. Normally, she would have been happy to see him, but this was no normal day. "What the devil can he want!" she scolded.

Chapter Six

From the doorway, she noticed Lord Harold was holding a blue vase, turning it upside down to read the name on the bottom. It was a Wedgwood vase with a figure in white relief showing the Apotheosis of Homer. Luten had given it to her for her birthday, spoiling the present by suggesting it might improve her taste. Harry was weighing it in the palm of his hand, looking about furtively, almost as if he planned to pocket it, only it was too large.

When he heard her approach, he set the vase down, smiling a welcome. Of all the deCoventrys, Harry was her favorite, indeed the only one she could like. It wasn't his dark good looks or his friendly way or the equality of their ages that appealed to her so much as his inferior position in the family. It lent him an uncertainty she could easily sympathize with. A younger son enjoyed few of the privileges of the reigning lord or his eldest son.

"Hello, Corrie," he said, with an abbreviated bow. "You're looking very stylish, as usual. Top of the trees. Speaking of top of the trees, how did Luten's masquerade go last night?" He showed her to the sofa and sat in the chair beside it.

"He made twelve thousand for Denise. Were you not there?"

"No, the price was too steep for me."

"You might have told me! I would have given you a ticket. It was for charity, after all."

"The lack of a ticket wouldn't have kept me away. I've

been to the Pantheon often enough that I know how to slip in the back door." His bright, intelligent eyes wore a quizzing look. "The truth is, Mama was enjoying one of her fits of the vapors, and I was assigned the task of bearing her company."

"The usual complaint?" Corinne asked.

"Precisely. Papa has a new flirt—Esmee Eskott, the redheaded actress from Drury Lane. An expensive chit, I hear. Mama's friends wasted no time in running to her with the news. It will cost Papa plenty to settle accounts. A diamond bracelet when he gives Esmee her congé, and something to soothe Mama's megrims. Or perhaps the deCoventry pearls will turn the trick with Mama. I do think it shabby of him to insist on your returning them."

A quiver of alarm jolted Corinne to attention. It was odd Harry had mentioned both the masquerade and the pearls within minutes of their meeting. Had he heard something? She sensed that Harry was looking at her very closely, but perhaps it was just embarrassment over the family quarrel about the pearls. She noticed, too, that deCoventry's new flirt performed at Drury Lane—and she was a redhead. An odd coincidence. Corinne went to pour wine, to give herself time to think.

"You should wear the pearls a few last times," he said, with a smile that appeared conspiratorial. "They look much better on you than on Mama. Of course it's Gaviston who put Papa up to it. He hopes to talk Papa into letting him give them to Lady Angela Gosse, to save buying her a wedding gift, the skint. His pockets are nearly as empty as mine, despite the generous allowance Papa gives him."

"Gaviston came to the sticking point? I hadn't heard it."

"Angela just accepted him this week. You'll be reading the announcement any day now. Cream pot love, of course. Lady Angela has a *dot* of twenty-five thousand."

"Surely Gaviston can't be in need of money. All those sinecures he's picked up in the House. He seems to be on every committee going. He's a cautious man. He doesn't gamble—does he?"

"Only for chicken stakes at Almack's. How he can tolerate that wax museum is beyond me. But then Gaviston has a pious streak in him. Never misses church on Sunday. Mind you, it's always the Chapel Royal. He likes to send his prayers to heaven in good company. No, he don't gamble. His vice is the common one of the deCoventrys. Women. He had a ladybird under his wing, Millie Winters, a pretty little blonde. He paid her off as soon as he started courting Angela. The Gosses are next door to Methodists. Those pious people always ferret out a fellow's sins. Think you're trying to poison their dog if you toss it a bone. They wouldn't approve of his having a mistress."

"Nor do I. Why would he need one, when he has Angela?"

He just looked his disagreement. "She's one of those dull, platter-faced gels. I daresay she'll suit Gaviston down to the heels. I prefer a little wickedness, myself."

They enjoyed a good coze. After half an hour, Harry rose and began twitching at his jacket in a way that indicated nervousness.

"Was there a special reason you called, Harry?" she asked.

"I feel a dashed beggar, but I wonder if you could lend me five pounds. I tried to borrow it from Gaviston, and got only a lecture for my pains. I owe Hoby for these boots I'm wearing. He won't give me the evening slippers I ordered until I pay him something on account. My old ones are falling apart."

"I can manage five." She occasionally acted as Harry's banker for small loans. He always repaid her, eventually.

She gave him the money and he said, "I'll repay you within the week. I shall run straight down to St. James's Street and retrieve my slippers for this evening. Many thanks, Corrie." He placed a quick kiss on her cheek and squeezed her fingers. She noticed his palms were rough.

He felt her touching them and said, "Rope burn. Hurts like the devil. I had a porker in a pig race last week. She lost by inches. I had trouble getting her to the starting post. She wanted to bolt on me. That's when I got this rope burn."

"I heard about the pig race."

"Well, thanks for the loan." He bobbed a bow and left.

Corinne sat on, thinking about his visit. The man who stole her pearls had had rough hands—but surely she would have recognized Harry? He had a cultured voice—unless he had changed it on purpose to fool her. Was it coincidence that he had mentioned both the masquerade and the pearls? It was natural that he should enquire about the former, and as the pearls were destined to change hands in a few days, then it wasn't unusual that he should mention them as well. Harry was all right. It was Gaviston and his mama who were greedy.

It was not for half an hour that she noticed a Meissen bonbon dish was missing from a side table. The dish was done in navy glaze with gilt trim, square-shaped, with a domed lid. It had been a parting gift from her sister Kate, and although it had little monetary value, she treasured it. Unlike the Wedgwood vase, it would fit easily into a pocket . . .

She asked Black to enquire of the servants if it had been broken. He was soon back to inform her Mary remembered it was on the table when she dusted that morning. Her servants didn't lie to her. She did not chastize them if they occasionally broke a dish. Harry must have taken it. He had been short of money, and planned to sell it. She felt betrayed.

Corinne had been invited to dinner with friends, but wrote to cancel the engagement, as she didn't know how long her meeting with Rose Grimm would take. At five o'clock, Luten came. His smile told her he had recovered from his fit of pique.

"I have my carriage waiting," he said. "The curricle is

too public. We'd be recognized. There's no point announcing our destination."

She put on her high-poked bonnet and they went out at once. Luten's passion was horses and carriages. Besides his curricle, his traveling carriage, and his landau with the crested panel, he also had a plain black carriage he used when he didn't care to be recognized. It was every bit as comfortable as his landau, with blue velvet squabs and silver appointments within. It was this carriage that waited at the curb. Prance called it his "hunting carriage," the inference being that it was used to hunt women, not foxes.

A yellow haze of fog and smoke from factories hung low over the city. They kept the windows closed to keep it out of their eyes and lungs. As they traveled east on Piccadilly, domes and towers pierced through the top of the haze, as if they were floating. The stately columns and pediments of the west end dwindled to the less polite precincts of Cranbourne Street, to the squalor of Long Acre. Luten's groom knew the city well; he had no difficulty finding Stukeley Street. When Corinne saw the run-down old brown brick mansion that had been turned into a rooming house, she was grateful for Luten's company. It was not the sort of place she would have felt safe venturing into alone.

The names of the occupants were pasted up in the hallway. Rose Grimm resided on the second story, in Room 2B.

"I'll go up with you and wait at the end of the hall," Luten said. "If there's a man with her, leave at once. Say you've gone to the wrong door. You're looking for—" He glanced at the list of occupants. "Edward Scrumm. But be sure you get a look at her caller."

"She'll recognize me," Corinne said.

Luten liked to be in charge. Every instinct protested against sending a lady into danger, but he knew Rose was more likely to talk to Corinne. "I'll be listening outside. Just shout if there's any trouble," he said.

She lifted her skirt as they climbed the dusty stairs, where balls of dust, scraps of paper and wizened apple cores were lodged against the rise. The stench of boiling cabbage and frying gammon filled the air. Somewhere a baby bawled disconsolately, as if it had cried for days, and knew its cries were in vain.

The notation 2B had been painted free hand on a varnished, unpaneled door. Luten went to the end of the hallway and Corinne raised her hand to knock, as there was no knocker. She knocked and waited, knocked again, while Luten looked a question, then came forward.

"She's not home," Corinne said.

Luten took hold of the door handle. It turned and the door opened. "She might have left a billet doux lying about."

Corinne demurred, but he walked boldly in. She peered down the hall before following him inside.

Chapter Seven

It was a room to stab her heart with pity. A simple truckle cot filled one corner. The washstand was a backless chair, on which rested a tin basin and a neatly folded piece of muslin that was obviously Rose's towel. A grate with a meager mound of cold ashes held a hanging kettle, with a fcw logs in a basket on the stone apron. A deal table and one chair sat by the window. The one cup, one plate, one fork and spoon on the table spoke of solitary meals. Bad as this was, it was Rose's attempts at beautifying the hovel that really caused Corinne to wince. The table was covered in an ell of richly embroidered material that was surely a remnant from some princely costume at the theater. A bouquet of paper flowers sat in a cup without a handle on the table. The stained walls held posters from the theater. There was no note from her lover, nor any diary to reveal her secret.

While Corinne gazed sadly about, Luten strode to the bed and returned with something in his hand. She saw that it was one of the arrows from Robin Hood's quiver. It was broken in half. Perhaps that was why Rose had removed it. They exchanged a meaningful look.

"Let us go," she said. "We'll wait for her belowstairs."

Luten glanced at his watch. "She should be here by now. It's nearly six o'clock. What's behind that curtain?" He gestured to a sheet, hung on a string at one side of the room.

"A cupboard? Or perhaps her clothes."

49

He went forward and drew the curtain aside. He stood for a moment, frozen, then quickly dropped the curtain.

"We'll leave now," he said in a wooden voice.

"What is it?" she demanded.

Something in his stricken expression caused the hair on her arms to lift. A spasm of fear jarred her heart. "Luten! It's not—" She took a pace toward the curtain.

He put out his hand and grasped her wrist. "Don't look," he said. He had only taken a quick peek himself, but it was enough to tell him that Rose would never reveal her secret. Her face was a horrible grayish-blue, with the eyes bulging out. A woman's stocking was tightly drawn around her neck.

Corinne wrenched her arm free and reached for the curtain. Through the opening slit she saw a few gowns hanging on a rod. And on the floor a crumpled body, with a tangled mass of blond hair partially concealing a distorted face that had once been palely pretty. A strangled gasp caught in Corinne's throat. A wave of nausea rose inside her, then a tremble shook her. She felt Luten's arms around her, drawing her warm and close against him. He cradled her in his arms until the trembling stopped.

"You shouldn't have looked," he said. "It will only give you nightmares."

"Luten, is she—is she—?"

"Yes, I'm afraid she is. Go home, Corinne. I'll notify Bow Street and wait here to learn what they discover."

Her eyes kept straying to the curtain. Luten held her head and turned it away from the awful sight. "How was she—"

"Strangled," he said curtly. "You go and wait for me in the carriage. I don't want you involved in this." As he spoke, he drew her out of the room and down the stairs.

"Are you sure she's dead? There's nothing we can do for her?" But of course she knew there was nothing more anyone could do for Rose Grimm except bury her decently.

"She's dead. We can only try to discover who killed her. You can drop me at Bow Street. I'll try to get hold of Townsend himself, let him know this crime isn't to be brushed aside because the victim is a nobody." He shook his head and gave a tsk. "That poor girl."

"I knew she was frightened. I thought it was of us, but it was him she was afraid of, her murderer. Oh this is all my fault! If I hadn't gone bothering her she might be alive."

As they reached the landing, a burly man in a soiled white shirt with a red kerchief at his throat came lumbering around the corner. He was six inches taller than Luten, who stood at six feet, and half again as broad. His thick neck and sloping shoulders gave him the appearance of a bear.

"Can I help you, sir?" he asked politely. "I'm Baxter. I take care of the place for Mr. Dooby, the landlord."

Luten paused a moment. He and Corinne had been seen descending the stairs. Corinne was as close to a fit of the vapors as made no difference. This giant would report their visit after the body was discovered, which would look suspicious. Best not to prevaricate.

"It seems one of your tenants has met with an accident," he said. "A fatal accident."

The man's eyes grew wide, while his face blanched. "Not Rose!" he exclaimed in a wild voice. "Not my Rosie!"

"Yes, Rose Grimm," Luten said gently. "I'm sorry." This would be the caretaker Phoebe had spoken of, who loved Rose.

"What happened? Did she fall?"

"No. It—it looks like murder."

Baxter turned to stone. For thirty seconds he just stood, staring into space, dumb with pain. Then he said, "Who dunnit? I'll kill him. I'll kill the bastard." He looked wild-eyed around the hall, as if expecting the murderer to be hiding there, then turned his furious stare on Luten.

Corinne feared for her companion and said, "It wasn't us. She was dead when we got there."

"I know it wasn't youse. Why would you kill the poor soul? I know who dunnit. Her fancy man. I told her he was trouble."

Before they could discover more about her "fancy man," Baxter bolted upstairs with Luten hot at his heels and Corinne lagging behind. Luten watched helplessly as Baxter looked all around the room, then headed unerringly to the curtain. He uttered an agonized, animal moan at what he saw there, then he gathered Rose's lifeless body into his arms, holding her to his breast, her blond hair falling over his fingers while he wailed in grief.

Luten said quietly over his shoulder to Corinne, "Ask my groom to send up the brandy I keep in the side pocket."

She was glad to be of use, and not sorry to escape the dreadful scene in the squalid little room. When she returned, Luten had got Baxter onto the chair and was trying to calm him down. She removed the dried flowers from the cup and poured two inches of brandy into it. She gave it to Luten, who handed it to Baxter. His teeth clattered against the cup when he raised it to his lips, but he drank deeply, without even wincing at the strong potion. When the cup was empty, he shook his head like a dog coming out of the water. His face had regained some color.

"Do you know the fancy man's name, Baxter?" Luten asked.

Baxter stared into the empty cup like a doomed man. "She'd never say his name. *M'sewer* she called him."

"Have you met him? Can you describe him to me?"

"I never met him. He's only been after her the last two weeks. Too swell for her to introduce to the likes o' me, but I seen him creeping up the stairs late at night like a tom cat. I told her he was up to no good, but she'd not hear it."

"What did he look like?"

"A little fellow. I could've broke his neck with one hand tied behind my back. I wish I'd done it."

"Dark hair, blond?"

Perhaps it was the thought of revenge that made Baxter suddenly look more animated. "Black as night. A good dresser. A gentleman. What a lady might call handsome, but no life in him. A face like a frozen mackerel. I only caught the odd peep of him from the corner of the hall."

"Did you see him arrive this evening?"

"I was in my kitchen. He don't usually come so early."

"Did you see him last night?"

"Aye, he come early last night as well, not this early but before dark, and left with a big package in his hand."

The costume! "Did he drive a carriage?"

"I doubt he walked all the way from wherever he lives. He ain't the sort to be living hereabouts, but he never come in a private carriage. A hired cab, usually. Last night he was on foot."

Luten stood a moment with his hand gripping Baxter's shoulder. "Did the man ever see you?"

"Nay. She wouldn't of liked it. Ashamed of knowing me, and all the while her great gent was planning to kill her."

"We'll find him, Baxter. I'm going to Bow Street. A Runner will come here. He'll want to ask you some questions."

"Bow Street bedamned. I'll find the bastard who done this to my Rosie. I'll kill him myself."

"We're leaving now," Luten said. He left the leather-covered bottle of brandy on the table.

When they were outside, he directed his groom to drive to Bow Street, planning to send Corinne on home in his rig. She sat, pale and shaken, beside him. His whole being ached for her pain. He wanted to draw her into his arms and comfort her.

"You mustn't blame yourself, Corinne," he said, taking her hand and squeezing her fingers.

53

"Why didn't I give deCoventry the pearls? What does a necklace matter compared to that poor girl's life? Why would anyone do such a thing? Rose would never harm a flea."

"No more she would. What concerns me is how the man knew we had found his costume. Rose must have told him we were asking about it at the theater, probably when he called on her this evening. It seems he didn't come prepared for murder, since he used one of her stockings. He knows we've discovered he wore that costume, and was afraid Rose would tell his name when it was learned he'd used the Robin Hood suit to steal the pearls. He could hang for it."

"If we had only gone half an hour earlier . . ."

"You mustn't blame yourself, or you'll sink into a decline. *You* didn't steal the pearls. *You* didn't kill Rose. All we can do for that unfortunate girl is discover who did kill her, and make sure he pays the price."

"Yes," she said, her chin firming to determination. "We must find him. This has gone beyond a string of pearls."

Luten spotted a passing hackney at the corner of Cranbourne and pulled the drawstring. "Go straight home. I'm going back to Rose's place with the Bow Street Runner to make a thorough search. I'll join you as soon as I can." He seized her hands and gazed at her with a concern so strong it looked like anger. "Don't let it prey on your mind, Corinne," he said gruffly. "We need all our wits to catch the bounder."

"Yes. Thank you, Luten, for everything."

He batted her thanks aside. "Take care." With his hand on the door handle, he stopped and reached his other hand out as if he would stroke her cheek. She waited, but he just gave her a ghost of a smile and withdrew his hand. "I'll be back soon," he said, and left.

Corinne found her thoughts wanted to linger on that gesture, that smile. She had to force herself to think how they could catch Rose's fancy man. It would help to atone for the awful knowledge that her insistence on wearing a necklace that didn't belong to her had caused the death of a helpless seamstress.

Chapter Eight

Coffen was at the window of his saloon, watching out for Corinne and Luten's return. He went to meet the carriage and accompanied her into her house, chatting about his visit.

"I cut the visit short. Miss Abercrombie was a snorting, romping lass—" He noticed Corinne was clinging to his arm for support, her cheeks as pale as winter grass. "But you ain't interested in Miss Abercrombie. Nor am I."

Prance was waiting in Corinne's Green Saloon, glancing through a copy of *Lady's Magazine* with some interest. He came darting out to meet them. As soon as they were inside, he called for wine, gently led Corinne to a sofa, arranged a petit point pillow at her back, and in an excess of enthusiasm, another beneath her feet. He thought it would look nice.

Coffen, who thought in terms of life rather than the stage, poured a glass of wine. "Have a gargle," he told her. "You'll feel better."

After a sip, she managed a weak thank-you to her helpers.

"My dear life," Prance said, bending over to hold her free hand, "what extraordinary event has brought you to this state? And why has Luten abandoned you in your hour of need? It will ease the pain to share it with us."

She looked at him with fear darkening her eyes and said, "Rose Grimm has been killed, and it's all my fault."

Prance flew to her defense. "That seamstress from

Drury Lane? A woman like that might have been killed by anyone."

"No, there was an arrow in her room."

Coffen screwed his face into a frown and said, "Indians!"

"No, no. It was one of Robin Hood's arrows."

"She's addled, poor girl," Coffen said in an aside to Prance. "Harking back to the masquerade. Robin Hood's been dead a few years—if he ever was alive."

"An arrow from the Robin Hood costume the thief wore last night," Prance explained, with unusual patience.

"Aha! The plot thickens! But I still don't see how—mean to say, Luten has the bow. Can't fire an arrow without a bow. Good God, you don't mean Luten killed her!"

Prance's small supply of patience was used up. "Oh do shut up and let Corinne tell the story."

She took another drink of wine and told them of her visit. They listened entranced, nodding and commiserating and asking a few questions.

When she had finished, Prance summed up the situation. "The thief-cum-murderer, let us call him Robin Hood for convenience's sake, had Rose smuggle the costume from Drury Lane for him. When he called on Rose this afternoon, she told him you had been at Drury Lane enquiring for the costume. He assumed you connected it, and him, with the robbery. Afraid that Rose would reveal his name, he killed her."

"Yes, that must be how it happened," Corinne agreed.

"Seems he has left us without a clue to our names," Coffen said, tugging at his ear. "Mean to say, Rose is dead. The only person who knows what he looks like is this fellow from Rose's rooming house, and he don't know the lad's name, or anything about him. Thing to do, we'll just have to wait until Robin Hood goes back to Rose's place and hope the man catches him."

"One assumes Robin Hood will avoid Stukeley Street in future," Prance said.

"Now there you're wrong. Killers always return to the scene of the crime," Coffen said. "I read it in a book."

"Only in fiction, Pattle."

"Eh?"

"In novels, not in real life."

"Is that so? P'raps we could lure him back somehow," was Coffen's next suggestion, but after a prolonged discussion, none of them could think how this might be done.

"What of the redheaded woman at the masquerade?" Corinne said. "If Rose was the man's *chère amie*, then who is she?"

"Red hair—she's a red hairing," Coffen concluded.

Prance looked pained. "And he's not even punning. Men have been known to have more than one *chère amie*, Pattle," he said. "One has only to think of our own royal dukes. Whoever the woman is, you may be sure she will keep well out of our way."

They next discussed what they would do that evening. Prance, never underestimating the group's importance, thought people would ask questions if they weren't seen about town.

"We don't want to behave in any unusual manner at this time. I've been besieged all day by friends demanding to know why we left the masquerade early. Rumors are adrift by now that the pearls are missing. We've been to every jeweler and fence in town enquiring after them. If deCoventry suspects the truth, he'll demand them at once. Much better to be seen out and in good spirits."

"You ask too much, Reggie," Corinne said in a weak voice.

"It is indeed a good deal to ask, but you are not alone, dear heart. How can we help you, if you won't help yourself?"

"Yes, you're right."

"And we must keep up our strength," Coffen added.

"Certainly," Prance agreed. "There is strength in numbers. We shall go *en masse* to the most glittering soirée that offers."

"I think Coffen means he's hungry," Corinne said, with a smile at Coffen. "Are you free for dinner this evening?"

"I was to dine at Aunt Agnes's," Coffen said. "Begged off when I got a look at Miss Abercrombie. I'm free."

"And I," Prance added. "I cleared my book of appointments to put myself entirely at your disposal, milady, including dinner this evening. Or would you prefer to dine *chez moi*? André is the most obliging creature in nature. He can throw us together a minor feast in the twinkling of a bedpost."

Coffen lifted his nose and sniffed the air like a hound. "I believe I smell roast beef, if my eyes don't deceive me."

Prance just shook his head.

"Cook is roasting a joint," Corinne assured him. "I hope you will both join me. Let us wait to see if Luten comes."

"No one civilized dines before eight," Prance declared.

"Deuce take it, it ain't even seven yet, and my stomach is growling," Coffen said, drawing out his watch.

Prance poked at his friend's bulging paunch and said, "You have enough lard to see you through a winter, Pattle. All this talk of food is beneath us. We have more important matters to discuss. Now, where do we go this evening? Does everyone have cards for the Duchess of Rowan's ball?"

"That'll be a dowdy do," Coffen objected. "It ain't a ball. It's a drum. Never attend a drum. They serve orgeat."

"I do draw the line at orgeat," Prance agreed.

Corinne said, "Let us wait to hear from Luten. Perhaps they have caught the man and we shan't have to go out at all."

"We still have to eat," Coffen said.

"Can't you subdue your fleshly appetites?" Prance scolded.

"What's that got to do with anything? Besides, I haven't had a woman in—"

"Let you and I go home and change for the evening, Pattle, while Corinne has a rest," Prance said, rather hastily. "She looks worn to the socket. No offense, dear heart, but if I may make an impertinent suggestion—just a *soupçon* of rouge on those damask cheeks *ce soir*."

"White as a sheet," Coffen added. "Starving to death."

"We shall return around eight," Prance said, drawing Coffen from the saloon.

Corinne was grateful for their help, but happy to have a few moments to herself. She found, however, that silence was even more enervating than their chatter. She had caught only a glimpse of Rose's body behind that curtain; imagination supplied the rest. She went above-stairs and changed for dinner.

"Have you found out anything about the pearls?" Mrs. Ballard asked.

Corinne told her the sad story. Mrs. Ballard was suitably shocked, but she had seen much of death at the country vicarage and knew all the consoling words to say. They didn't really help.

As it seemed possible that Corinne would have to drag herself off to a party that evening, she chose one of the new gowns she had had made up for the season. George had liked her to wear pastel gowns, but since his death she had graduated to more mature hues. She chose a deep blue gown in Italian crepe, with lace inserts in the skirt. Mrs. Ballard drew her raven hair back from her face, held behind with jeweled combs. She added diamond ear drops and necklace to complete the ensemble.

When Mrs. Ballard had left, Corinne drew a rouge pot from the back of her drawer and carefully applied rouge to her cheeks, for she looked like a ghost. Her eyes were haunted with shadows, but at a quick glance her appearance was well enough.

As she descended to the saloon, the door knocker sounded peremptorily. Luten! She darted downstairs and met him as Black showed him in. Eagerness lent a sparkle to her eyes, and her elegant toilette suggested that she had recovered from the afternoon's shock. They went straight into the saloon.

"Any news?" she demanded at once.

He shook his head. "Townsend and I went over Rose's room carefully. We questioned her neighbors. None of them could help us. It's highly unlikely the man will return to her room. We must discover some other way of finding him."

They held their conversation standing in the middle of the saloon.

"The redhaired woman who was with him last night knows who he is. He might kill her as well. We should warn her, Luten. Place an advertisement in the journals, or—"

Luten realized that what he took for high spirits was closer to hysteria. His heart wrenched to see her so troubled. He spoke calmly, to soothe her. "They're likely in it together. She wouldn't respond to an advertisement."

Her shoulders slumped. "I expect you're right. Reggie feels we all ought to go out this evening, to prevent talk in case deCoventry twigs to it that the pearls are missing—all our questioning around town, you know. That's why I've dressed. They're coming here for dinner. I hope you can join us."

Luten had planned to invite her to his house for a quiet dinner, just the two of them. He had been looking forward to it, but Prance's idea was, in fact, a good one.

"Yes, I'll come. We must go out later, of course. I wonder where one might encounter the French set this evening."

"The French? Why do you think they might be involved?"

"Why, because of what Rose called her lover."

"But she didn't call him by name."

61

"Baxter said she called him *M'sewer*."

"*Monsieur?* I didn't hear him say that."

"You were—preoccupied. He said it, and repeated later when I questioned him again that the man was French. 'Him with his *bonjours* and *au revoirs*,' he said. It's not much of a clue, but it's the only one we have at the moment."

"But the man who stole my pearls didn't have a French accent."

"You were upset, and he only said a few words."

"I doubt he'll be at a polite party. I had the notion the man was not quite a gentleman. His voice was uncultured."

"That might be because English is not his first language," Luten suggested.

"I suppose it could be that, or he might have been changing his voice. His hands were rough, too." She thought of Harry, and his story of rope burn. There *had* been a pig race in Hyde Park, though.

"How rough?" Luten asked, frowning in concentration. "You saw him, spoke to him. Is there anything else you remember?"

"It was dark and crowded at the Pantheon. He didn't speak at all until he was leaving. I mistook him for you, so we are looking for a Frenchman about your size. That's strange, too. Baxter called him a little fellow, but you're not small. Is it possible there are two men involved?"

"I shouldn't think so. Baxter is next door to a giant. I fancy he'd call me a little fellow. What about the man's hands? Were they rough all over, or just calloused, as a hard rider's might be roughened from holding the reins?"

Corinne closed her eyes and tried to remember. "I didn't actually notice their appearance. His fingers on my throat felt rough." She opened her eyes and shook her head. "I don't know. It all happened so quickly."

"Would you recognize him if you saw him again?"

"No, I don't think I would."

"I hope he realizes that," Luten said, frowning.

"Why? What do you—" She gave a gasp. The man had killed Rose Grimm because she could identify him. "Oh I'm sure he doesn't fear me. He could have killed me at the masquerade if that was what he had in mind. His hands were at my neck. All he had to do was tighten his fingers." Her fingers went to her neck. A shiver trembled through her as she realized how vulnerable she had been. How vulnerable Rose had been . . .

As the blood drained from her face, Luten noticed the two pink blots of rouge on her cheeks. Corinne, sunk to rouging her cheeks! The poor girl was close to exhaustion, kept going by anxiety. And there was little he could do to help her.

He spoke confidently, but a pinching at the corner of his lips betrayed his fear. "We shan't let anything happen to you, Corinne. Don't leave this house without one of us for escort. The worst that can happen is that you have to pay deCoventry for the pearls. I wager he'd take those diamonds you're wearing in exchange, without selling your estate, or dipping into your capital."

"I'm not worrying about *money*, Luten!" she said angrily.

Offended by her attack, he snapped, "You should be!"

"How can you think me so greedy? It's Rose I'm thinking of." Tears swelled in her eyes. She didn't know whether she had pitched herself into Luten's arms, or he had drawn her into them. She only knew he was holding her close, and it felt so wonderfully safe and warm there that she never wanted to leave.

"I'm so fortunate to have you," she said, sniffling back her tears.

Luten's heart jumped in delight. At that moment, there was no doubt in his mind or heart whether he loved the countess or hated her. When he spoke, his voice was husky. "Corinne, my dear girl. You know you can always count on me."

"You've all been so kind. You and Reggie and Coffen."

His pleasure dwindled as he realized her meaning. "We'll all help you to the utmost of our ability," he said, loosening his arms and stepping back.

She drew away from him, wiping at her moist eyes. "What a perfect ninnyhammer you must think me. I want to see that Rose has a proper burial. Who would I speak to about that?"

"Those details have been taken care of already. I've spoken to Mr. Wilson, from the theater. Rose has a family in Ilford. They've been notified. Her body will be sent home for a decent burial, with her friends attending."

"I want to pay for it."

"That's been taken care of."

"By you! At least let me share the cost. Show me the bill when it comes. And now you must run home and change for dinner. The others will be back soon. Prance said eight o'clock."

"Take care." This time, he did touch her cheek lightly, before leaving. It felt fevered, yet she was shivering.

Chapter Nine

To Lady deCoventry's astonishment, her impromptu dinner party was a success. She always enjoyed these informal dos with her closest friends. They reminded her of Ireland, and home. At larger parties, she usually found herself partnered on one side by some superannuated politician, and on the other by a flirt. Society considered the Berkeley Brigade so close to a family that they separated them at the dinner table.

That evening, her hostessing duties provided a welcome distraction from more pressing worries, but even before they sat down, she had decided she must clear her head of futile repinings to devote herself to the job at hand. Worrying would not bring back Rose, but the pearls were out there in someone's pocket, and she meant to get them back.

As the guests were so few, she had dinner served in the morning parlor, where she didn't have to bother about which gentleman to seat at the foot of the table. The table was round. Luten sat at her right hand, Coffen at her left, with Prance and Mrs. Ballard across from her. Corinne watched with a calming sense of familiarity as Prance applied his knife and fork to a pickle and Coffen snabbled down his roast beef.

Luten told the others about Rose calling Robin Hood *M'sewer*, which suggested he was French. "What we have to decide is where we might find him this evening," he said. "Any ideas?"

"Those émigrés tend to show up at embassy parties,"

Prance replied, "but I don't believe there is one tonight. One of the other ambassadors' wives might be having a private do. Countess deLieven, Princess Esterhazy," he said, naming the Russian and Austrian ambassadorial spouses, who were both prominent in society.

Corinne sent a footman off for her invitations. She flipped through them. "Nothing from either of them. Wait! Here's something! The Castlereaghs."

"They ain't French," Coffen said. "The name sounds like it, but they're English as John Bull."

"Irish, actually," Prance said, spearing a pea on the tine of his fork and examining it suspiciously. "But as Castlereagh is the foreign secretary, he's on close terms with the ambassadors and other foreigners. If our Robin Hood is a French gentleman—which is not at all certain, by the by—then it's possible he'll be at Castlereagh's ball."

"Stands to reason," Coffen agreed. "If he's a French aristo, his pockets are to let. Bound to be plenty of well-dowered ladies at the ball. The émigrés are all scrambling for an heiress, since their revolution stole their estates from them. Poor blighters. Which is not to say I approve of them stealing Corinne's pearls."

Corinne had an unsettling feeling that they were going off on a tangent. The man hadn't spoken with a French accent; he didn't even sound like a gentleman. And what of his redheaded friend? It was by no means sure she had been his accomplice. She might have no idea he'd stolen the pearls. And even if she had helped him, that didn't guarantee her safety. Rose Grimm had helped him by providing the costume, and she was dead. Corinne had already mentioned the redhead more than once. The others listened politely, then continued their conjecturing as if she hadn't spoken. A mere lady was ignored when important business was being discussed.

Luten, as the head of the gang, took it upon himself to decide that Castlereagh's was their destination. He also arranged their transportation. "We shall each take our own carriage, in case we want to follow various suspects."

"Corinne shouldn't go alone. Robin Hood might get hold of her," Coffen said.

"The countess will come with me," Luten replied. Prance gave him a knowing look but didn't object. Nor did Corinne.

As the dinner party was informal, the ladies were invited to remain at the table while the gentlemen took their port. To repay their kindness, Corinne allowed them to smoke their cheroots. Prance, who did not smoke, assured her it was an honor to forgo the pleasure. Coffen helped himself to a cheroot from the humidor on the sideboard.

"I shall take snuff," Prance announced, drawing out a new snuffbox and offering it around. He didn't usually take snuff, but he liked pretty trinkets. "I had the box made to my own design. Cloisonné. The pattern is a detail from my family's crest. A lion passant, in gold on a black ground. Not really a spring box, but it's rather amusing."

Luten declined and took his own sort. He passed Prance's box along to Coffen, who looked at the box and took a pinch of snuff. He inhaled it along with the cigar smoke and began a series of smoky sneezes, every one of which Mrs. Ballard greeted with, "God bless you."

"Throw a glass of port on him, Luten. I believe he's caught fire," Prance said.

Coffen peered at them through watery eyes and gulped down a glass of port. "What do you put in that snuff? It tasted like toilet water."

"A drop of lavender water, to keep it moist," Prance said.

After port, the gentlemen made a dart home to pick up their invitations, then left for Castlereagh's in a caravan at nine o'clock. The smoke and haze of afternoon had thickened to an earth-bound cloud that made vision nearly impossible and necessitated a slow pace to avoid accidents. The only evidence that the streets were crowded was the softly diffused carriage lamps, and the clatter of wheels and hooves over the cobblestones. Carriages were lined up for two blocks at Castlereagh's house, awaiting entry. Torches had been lit outside to welcome the guests and light their way to the door. A bevy of liveried footmen were in attendance, ready to render assistance.

The guests were announced and entered the ballroom, to be greeted by the foreign secretary and his wife. Castlereagh, who knew the Clares in Ireland, treated Corinne as a sort of daughter.

"Lady deCoventry," he said, placing a kiss on her cheek. "Delighted you could come. You have completed the deCoventry contingent. You'll find your relatives somewhere about the place. Lord Harry was enquiring for you. I was telling Lady deCoventry how helpful her elder son is to me. The soul of discretion. Gaviston did excellent work for us in Vienna with Metternich. His grasp of foreign languages is admirable. We have no shortage of those who can speak French, but German! That lad will be an ambassador before he's much older. He must be a great relief to his papa. The younger lad— well, I don't have to tell *you*. An expensive fribble. A sad vexation to his papa. We must use our influence to straighten him out."

Luten kept a jealous watch on the dashing foreign secretary, who was said to have an eye for the ladies. He stepped forward and shook Castlereagh's hand before Corinne could reply.

"Your relatives!" he said in a sardonic undertone when they were free of the host. "An unexpected pleasure."

"I expected Gaviston would be here. I'm surprised Harry was invited, since Castlereagh has such a low opinion of him."

"Not unwarranted," Luten said.

Corinne remembered Harry's visit, and the missing Meissen box. She shook the shred of doubt away. Harry might snitch a trifling object but he wouldn't steal her pearls, and he would certainly never kill anyone. They entered the ballroom, to be confronted with a swirling mass of people, a cloud of perfume and a cacophony of sound. The opening minuet was just finishing. Ladies in colored silks and satins stood out like exotic flowers against the gentlemen's darker jackets. Lamplight caught the glitter of diamonds and rubies, the duller flicker of gold. The feathers in the ladies' turbans rose like a fairy forest to flirt with the dangling chandeliers overhead. Lady Melbourne's plumes were in some danger of igniting.

Countess deLieven came bustling forward, drawn not by Lady deCoventry but by the dashing Lord Luten. This lady, while making only a small claim to beauty, was popular because of her liveliness and wit, and her close friendship to Prinney. She wore her black hair in an unsightly twist of tight curls sticking out at odd angles, as if she had just removed the curling papers and not bothered to brush her hair.

"What a squeeze!" she exclaimed merrily. "Half of Europe is here. I have not seen such an unruly mob since Prinney convinced me it was my duty to go to the ladies' chamber to watch a session of Parliament. Shocking the way you fine lords have at each other, Luten. At least you all speak English. This is a regular Tower of Babel. I've counted six different languages."

Luten bowed and complimented her on her ugly puce gown and enviable emeralds. Then he said, "In which corner of the room would one hear French spoken?"

"You want to avoid it, I wager," she said roguishly. "One must pity the émigrés, but really they are becoming a bore, always pestering one for a post. The Duchesse de Nance is in the card room. I saw the Conte d'Armiens chasing after Miss Dewar. A butter-toothed chit, but a great fortune, of course."

"There is one particular gentleman I'm looking for," he said. "Unfortunately I don't know his name. He

69

assisted Lady deCoventry when her horse got away from her on Rotten Row, and she wanted to thank him."

"Fear not, he will call on her. They use the slightest pretext to get a foot in the doorway."

"It was two days ago, and he hasn't called."

"Indeed?" She turned to Corinne. "What did he look like?"

"He was about Luten's size, dark hair," she replied.

Countess deLieven gave a hard stare. "Handsome, was he? You can do better than a disinherited Frenchie, my dear. What is wrong with Luten, if it is a *mari* you are after? I don't know any Frenchies as tall as Luten. They're usually runtish, don't you agree? Look at Bonaparte . . ." She shrugged her bony shoulders dismissingly.

Corinne decided to try a different tack. "He was with a tall redheaded lady," she said. "They were together at Luten's charity masquerade party for Denise. Were you there?"

"I wouldn't have missed it! Odd the host played truant. Yes, I noticed a striking redhead, but she wasn't with a Frenchie when I saw her. She was with Robinson."

"Did she wear a black domino and feathered mask?"

"That's her. I wager Robinson could put you onto her, and she could steer you to the Frenchie—if you are that eager to thank him."

"Who is this Robinson?" Corinne asked.

"A fellow who does dirty work for gentlemen. All the embassies use him for personal jobs. Don't smirk, milord!" she said to Luten. "The lads at your foreign office are very familiar with him as well. He has a broad clientele—anyone who can pay his price, and he don't come cheap. Surely you know Robinson, Luten?"

"Why, Countess, you must know the Whigs don't involve themselves in dirty work."

"Ha! And England never sees a cloud. If you ever need a good man, try Robinson. The very soul of discretion. He's a carpenter by trade; calls himself a restorer of antiques, but he is actually a forger. He 'restored' that lovely little Chippendale desk in Castlereagh's front hall. Margaret found the knobs in her attic, and he attached the desk to them. A clever scoundrel, and carpentering is not his only skill. He will steal letters or follow a straying husband—or wife. Sell you a deck of shaved cards and steer you to a game for deep stakes. Oh yes, Robinson is up to every rig and racket in town. Petty jobs, you know. Mind you, he is a loyal Englishman. He doesn't do spy work against his own. He absolutely refused—but you aren't interested in that."

"Where would we find him?" Corinne asked. It had occurred to her that a carpenter would have rough hands, and as the ball had been held at the Pantheon, anyone with the price of a ticket could attend.

"His shop is in Shepherd's Market, south of Curzon Street. There's a sign in the window. He lives over the shop."

"What does he look like?" she asked.

"You'll recognize him. He works alone. There won't be anyone else there. He's a tall, strapping fellow. Dark hair." Lady deLieven looked away as she spoke. She had just spotted her arch rival, Lady Jersey, and wanted to see what she was wearing, and whose husband she was stealing. "Nice chatting to you," she said. "Go after Robinson. He'll help you out." Then she left.

"Interesting," Luten said. "We'll give Robinson a try tomorrow."

"Let us go some place quiet where I can think."

They left the ballroom and strolled down a marble-floored hall to the library, where a few guests had sought peace amidst the rows of leather-bound tomes. They went to an unoccupied loveseat that gave them privacy.

"Luten, the thief we are calling Robin Hood didn't have a French accent—but he had rough hands, like a carpenter," Corinne said. "Lady deLieven saw Robinson with the redhead. He's tall and dark. I think he stole the pearls."

"Nonsense. I know Robinson. He's only a petty crook.

71

He wouldn't be involved in anything like murder. The man who took your pearls only said a few words. You were upset—you didn't catch his accent. A carpenter is hardly a gentleman. Rose made much of her beau being a fine gent, you recall. A French gent. We don't actually know that the woman Countess deLieven saw with Robinson was our redhead."

Corinne wasn't convinced. "She wore the same outfit."

"There were plenty of black dominoes at the do. It's worth looking into, but while we're here, let us circulate and try to get a line on *Monsieur*."

She sensed that he was just humoring her. They were at the doorway of the library when they spotted Lord Gaviston and Lady Angela Gosse coming toward them.

"Oh lord," Corinne said. "There's no escape. I hope he doesn't ask me to dance."

Chapter Ten

"Cuz!" Lord Gaviston exclaimed, drawing up beside Lady deCoventry. He was taller than average, slightly built, but with good shoulders. No one had ever accused him of being a dandy. His jacket, while well cut, was modest. His shirt points came nowhere near his ears, and the diamond in his cravat was no larger than a petit pois. He wore his dark hair barbered close to his head. Except for a more than usually long chin, his face was undistinguished. It was caught somewhere between the bonhomie of his papa and the spiteful malice of his mama.

"Not out leading the dance?" he said to Corinne. "It's unlike you to sequester yourself in a library. Lady Castlereagh must have a good supply of gothic novels." He gave the sort of loud laugh that indicated a gentleman ill at ease with a lady.

It gave one pause to think that he was one of the government's more able diplomats.

"Gaviston," she replied, with a small curtsey. Then she turned to greet Lady Angela.

Corinne used to wonder what lady could ever find Gaviston attractive enough to marry him. The day she met Lady Angela, her question was answered. She was cut from the same bolt as his mama. She was tall and handsome enough at a glance, but possessed not an iota of charm. Her broad, pink cheeks lent her a vacuous look that her sharp green eyes belied. The word about London was that she would marry a yahoo if he had a title and fortune. Viscount Gaviston would one day be an earl like her dear papa. She had gone after him buckle and thong, and got him screwed to the sticking place within weeks.

"I hear congratulations are in order," Corinne said.

"Surely congratulations to Gaviston. One wishes the bride-to-be well," Lady Angela replied, with great condescension.

"Of course," Corinne murmured, willing down the retort that it was condolences she should be offering Gaviston.

"Do you think it quite the thing for you and Luten to be slipping off into dark corners, my dear?" Lady Angela said. "A widow like yourself must be careful of her reputation."

Gaviston saw that his beloved was offending Luten. He said, "The pot calling the kettle black, my dear. We're here ourselves."

"It's hardly the same thing. We are engaged."

"It is well to maintain a show of propriety—as well as the real thing, of course," he agreed at once.

A few polite nothings were exchanged. Luten pointedly congratulated both of them. Lady Angela did not repeat her lesson in etiquette, but smirked triumphantly, well pleased with her catch.

"Well, Cuz," Gaviston said, "we don't see you often enough. You must join a new charity I am involved in—a home for unwed mothers. More sinned against than sinning, really."

"I didn't see you at my charity ball," Luten said, to get Corinne off the hook.

"Papa doesn't allow me to go to the Pantheon," Lady Angela announced. "So déclassé."

Gaviston nodded in approval. "Masks do tend to lower the morals. A sad comment on humankind. Actually, a friend of Angela's had a little engagement party for us last night, so I couldn't have gone to your masquerade in any case."

"Lady Chatham," Lady Angela informed them. "The party was not that small. Two dozen sat down to dinner;

74

twenty more joined us later for an impromptu rout. All younger couples, like ourselves. Mama will be inviting you both to our formal engagement party next week."

Gaviston said, "Oh, by the by, Luten, I left a note on your desk this afternoon. Castlereagh wants to know—unofficially—if you Whigs are planning to fight us on that Austrian business."

"To the death, Gaviston," Luten replied. "But let us not discuss politics at a ball, or we shall come to cuffs."

"He is always thinking of work," Lady Angela said nobly.

During a brief pause, Gaviston said to Corinne, "Will you stand up with me, Cuz?"

Bereft of an excuse, she went to the ballroom with him, leaving Luten to partner Lady Angela. They were in the same set for the cotillion. At every opportunity, Luten glared at Corinne for subjecting him to this unpleasant interlude. As soon as it was over, he took her arm and led her away.

"Someone should put a muzzle on that bitch," he said.

Before she could enquire what Angela had said, Lord Harold came smiling up to them.

"I see you got stuck to stand up with the lovebirds," he said, and laughed. "Angela ain't speaking to me this evening, thank God. I failed to attend her party last night. A dashed insult. I'm Gaviston's brother and she only invited me to the dance after dinner. I could have gone; Mama was asleep by ten, but I took a snit and stayed away. Gaviston must have lost his wits, offering for that old bint. Mutton dressed as lamb."

Not wanting to disparage the lady in public, Corinne replied, "She will keep him on the straight and narrow."

"Gaviston hardly needs help in that direction. He wouldn't recognize the garden path if he fell down it. I am the black sheep of the family. But she will certainly keep him on a short leash. I say, would you like to help me break in my new slippers?" He held up a foot to show her what her loan had accomplished. "After all, you paid for them."

Luten's ears perked up at this. He knew of Corinne's fondness for Lord Harry. He knew, as well, that Harry was hanging out for a well-dowered wife. The deCoventrys would like very well to see her property back in the family. Corinne, pleased at the tokens of jealousy she saw in Luten's stiff face, accepted his offer.

As soon as Luten left, Harry said, "The fact is, I wanted to get you alone for a minute. No, don't pull that Friday face on me, Corrie. I ain't going to dun you for another loan. The fact is . . ." He paused, embarrassed. "Your Meissen box—I borrowed it. I'm sorry. I have it in my pocket this minute. I shall give it back to you this very night. I picked it up before you came in this afternoon. I didn't think you'd mind. After I got away I recalled you're especially fond of it. I wanted to replace it when you lent me the money, but I was afraid you'd see me. Then I was afraid you would miss it, and know I had taken it. I was only going to hawk it and return it later. I've been feeling as guilty as sin about it."

"That box does have a special meaning for me, Harry. I don't mind lending you a little something when you're caught short, but don't take things again."

"I was only borrowing it! You know I ain't a thief, Corrie! Dash it, I lived in your house for a year, and nothing was taken. When I broke that little French vase, I told you about it. I offered to replace it. Anyone might break a vase. I'm sorry I took the box," he said, with his head hanging in shame. "You're the only relative I actually like. It would be too bad if I managed to turn you against me as well."

"I'm not turned against you. Far from it. But if you don't mind, we shan't stand up for the next dance. I—I am looking for someone," she said vaguely.

"So am I. Some undemanding lady in need of a penniless husband. Can you recommend anyone?"

"I'll keep my eyes open," she said.

"Can you take this now?" He handed her the Meissen box. She felt again the rough prickle of his fingers. Rougher than the thief's, weren't they? Harry's roughness was due to broken blisters, with the skin drying. Quite a sharp prickle. Though he was the right size and shape . . .

As she slipped the box into her reticule he said, "I'm sorry, Corrie. I'll not do it again."

"It's forgotten," she said, and wished it were true.

She had come to this ball in the hope of discovering *Monsieur*, and looked about for a possibility. Prance, resplendent in a mulberry jacket, drifted up to her. He wore a bored look, but his eyes held a gleam.

"I've lined up a prospect," he said in a stage whisper. "There's a group of émigrés in the refreshment parlor, swilling down punch. To think the French have fallen to that! They're all dark-haired; one of them is about Luten's size. If you roll your eyes at him, he won't be tardy in coming forward. I managed to scrape an acquaintance. He calls himself the Conte de Creuse. When I mentioned carpets, he looked perfectly blank. The same way you are looking now, my sweet ignoramus. Aubusson is in the *département* of Creuse. It is famous for its carpets and tapestries."

"I've heard of Aubusson carpets!"

"I doubt Aubusson has ever heard of this *conte*."

He hustled her off to the refreshment parlor where four forlorn gentlemen in outmoded jackets and bad haircuts stood around the punch bowl, muttering in low voices as they eyed the heiresses. The tall one was the most handsome of the lot. He had the flashing eyes and dark good looks of the Latin. When Corinne smiled, he made an exquisite bow. Within thirty seconds he was darting forward.

"Ah, Countess, allow me to introduce a new friend, the Conte de Creuse," Prance said.

The *soi-disant conte* bowed punctiliously and expressed himself *enchanté*. He had heard much of the

77

countess's beauty—and her prowess on the dance floor. While his three companions watched in envy, he led her out of the refreshment parlor, clinging to her elbow as if she planned to bolt on him.

"This is most incredible good fortune!" he exclaimed. *"La valse!"* Then he drew her into his arms and began whirling her around the floor with great dexterity, while simultaneously showering her with compliments.

She danced like Terpsichore. He understood madame was a widow, was it not so? Her hair, of the most exquisite gentleness putting crows to shame. And did madame live with her husband's family? Her own house! *Très commode, cela.* He missed his vast estates in Creuse. How madame would have enjoyed to see his rolling vineyards, stretching to the horizon. One day he would have them back, *certainement.* Her flesh, like unto the ivories and damasks. And how he missed his home! Now, alas, he had not even a proper domicile. He was filled with shame to invite madame to a little *assemblage* of a few friends *chez lui* after this evening's ball. Around midnight. Perhaps madame would deign to honor him?

"I couldn't go alone," she said.

Mais absolument! Madame must bring her friends, including lady friends. A little wine, a little conversation. She was too kind. At midnight, then. He gave her the address, a cottage on the banks of the Thames, not far from Whitehall.

The *conte* wore a broad smile when he rushed back to inform his fellow *contes* of his grand success. A veritable fortune! And though the lady lacked conversation, she was neither ugly nor ancient.

Corinne went in search of Luten to report on the *conte,* and to ask him to accompany her to his cottage.

Luten was in a testy mood. "That wasn't Harry you were standing up with. Who was it? He looked like a caper merchant."

"It was the Conte de Creuse. A tall, dark Frenchman," she said, giving him a pointed look.

"That's what I thought," he said, hoping to conceal his jealousy.

"I can't believe he is the man who stole my pearls. Those hands have never held anything rougher than a wine glass, but he says there will be several of his friends at his cottage. We might meet *Monsieur*."

"Excellent. Invite Prance and Coffen as well. I've been thinking about Robinson. I'll have a word with him tonight."

"Good!"

"Happy to be rid of me, eh?" he said archly.

"No, but I do feel Robinson is Robin Hood, and the sooner we find him, the better."

"I'll slip out and go at once."

"I could go with you." She read a glint of interest in his eyes, a look of satisfaction that she wanted to be with him.

"You'd best follow up on *M'sewer*. We want to cover all possibilities. I'll try to meet you back here before you go off with the Frenchies." Corinne gave him the address, in case she had already left.

"If nothing comes of all this, I'll have another go at Drury Lane tomorrow," he said. "Rose may have confided about her lover to someone at the theater."

"Fine. Oh dear, here comes deCoventry!"

A gentleman with silver hair and blue eyes was advancing, drawing with him a portly dame in a gown of Olympian blue. A riot of flesh strained at the bodice of her gown, nearly swallowing a handsome set of sapphires that Corinne had used to be especially fond of.

"My dear," deCoventry said, bowing. He avoided using Corinne's title, as it vexed his wife. "Lovely to see you again. We don't see enough of you. You never come to call."

"I'm sure the door is always open," Lady deCoventry declared, in a self-righteous tone.

"I hear Gaviston has become engaged," Corinne said, to change the subject. She did feel delinquent, but her visits to her old home were uncomfortable. The last time she had called, Lady deCoventry had sat with her for half an hour without volunteering a word, only answering questions. She hadn't offered a cup of tea, or even a glass of wine. The lady was known to be religious. She had managed to instill her strict principles in Gaviston, but Harry (and her husband) had rebelled.

"Lady Angela," Lady deCoventry said. "A lovely gel. A real lady," she added, with a sharp look at the Irish hoyden.

Corinne saw Luten bristle up. Before he could speak, deCoventry said, "Irene has had enough of jigging for one night." Irene was his wife. "I am looking for Harry to take her home. I must stay a little longer. Mustn't offend Castlereagh, when Gaviston has to work with him. Castlereagh has a high opinion of Edward."

"He spoke very highly of Gaviston," Corinne said.

Lady deCoventry's sour face eased into a smirk. "And it is not only his work in Parliament. He is active in half a dozen charities besides. On boards of directors, you know. Always working for the good of others. A real Christian."

Her husband was looking around the room. "Where has young Harry got off to, the scamp?"

"I'll have a look in the refreshment parlor," Corinne offered. She and Luten made their escape.

"Of course deCoventry has no intention of staying here," Corinne said, as they went in search of Harry. "He'll head straight to Drury Lane."

"With a wife like that, who can blame him?"

"His Esmee is a redhead, by the by."

"Yes, but not *our* redhead. She was performing last night. I noticed a review of the play in the *Morning Observer*."

They found Harry, not in the refreshment parlor, but with a pack of bachelors, ogling the debs from the side of the room. Corinne gave him his papa's message.

"Time for Papa's date with Esmee, is it?" he said.

He turned to his friends. "I shall be back in two shakes. Wait here for me." Then he went off to deliver his mama home.

Luten handed Corinne over to Coffen and went in search of Mr. Robinson. At midnight, the Conte de Creuse reminded Corinne of his party. She got Coffen to accompany her. Prance was to remain at the ball to see what he could learn.

Chapter Eleven

When Corinne entered the ramshackle little cottage on the Thames, she felt the Conte de Creuse's worst crime was his poverty. The reason society disliked the French émigrés was their dangling after the heiresses, but if that were a crime, half the English aristocracy would be in Newgate. The party consisted of the four French *'contes,'* Coffen, Corinne, two inferior bottles of red wine and a plate of cheese and biscuits. The four French gentlemen lived together in the small, dank cottage. The dearth of belongings suggested they were not involved in any theft except for the mismatched pieces of cutlery and china bearing the imprint of various hotels. Thieves would not be wearing jackets with threadbare cuffs, unless they were exceedingly inept thieves.

They had decided amongst themselves that Lady de-Coventry belonged to the Conte de Creuse. He led her to a well-worn sofa in the corner of the parlor, while Coffen was entertained on the far side of the room by the other three. It hardly allowed privacy as the parlor was only fifteen feet long. Corinne heard once again that her hair was of the most exquisite gentleness, putting, this time, ravens to shame. Her flesh—surely he meant skin—continued its ivory/damask purity, and her eyes had taken on the lustre of the *emeraudes*. She was so busy fighting off his flattery that it was impossible to quiz him.

She hoped Coffen was making more headway with questioning the other three. The *conte* had only one arrow in his quiver: romance. After half an hour, Coffen said that the Conte de Muraille was going to show him a set of medals given to him by some ancestor, and left the room with the other three *contes*. At this point, de Creuse hastened his courtship. He put a tentative arm around Corinne's shoulder and confessed that he had always had a *tendresse* for lovely young widows. She assumed the others had drawn Coffen away to allow the *conte* to make his move, and perhaps to try to sell Coffen the medals.

Luten drove through the fog along fashionable South Audley Street to Curzon. Lanterns blazed at a few houses, indicating a party was in progress there. Music wafted through one open doorway to confirm it. A few carriages passed, coming to or leaving the parties. He turned the corner and was suddenly in another world. There was no traffic in the dark, narrow laneway that opened before him. Decrepit buildings pushed close to the road on either side. Most of them were commercial establishments: small manufactures, antique shops and pawn shops. At midnight, there were only two windows lit. They cast wan puddles of light on the cobblestones. He had the carriage stopped in front of one of the lighted windows. By the lamps from his carriage he read the name on the hanging sign. R. J. ROBINSON, ANTIQUES RESTORED. A restored Tudor chest with an intricate marquetry lining was in the window as a sample of his work.

A glance in the window showed the shop was vacant. One lamp burned low. The oil in its base was nearly gone. He doubted that Robinson would go away and leave a lamp burning. When he knocked at the door, there was no reply. He knocked again, setting his other hand on the door handle to try it. The door opened inwards.

"Mr. Robinson!" he called. "Anyone here?" Receiving no reply, he stepped in and confirmed that no one was in the shop. Tables, chairs, chests and dressers in various stages of repair (or construction) were ranged helter-skelter about the jumbled room. One desk, the one with the lamp burning, was no antique but a serviceable deal work table holding a welter of papers, indicating that it was Robinson's personal desk.

Luten knew he'd have no chance to search it once Robinson arrived. He looked quickly through the pile of invoices and query letters, then slid open the drawer. Robinson kept no record of his criminal activities. There were two account books, one for his legitimate antique restoring business, the other a list of customers who were interested in gambling, with their preferred game. He returned the ledgers, closed the drawer and called again. Still there was no reply.

As Robinson lived above the shop, Luten figured he had stepped up to his apartment. He lit a taper from the lamp and advanced toward a box staircase at the rear of the shop on the left, wedging his way around a mahogany table, calling as he went.

"Mr. Robinson! Are you up—" The last word died in his throat. He felt something under his foot. He looked down. There, at the bottom of the stairs, lay Robinson with a dark stain on his shirt front. Luten had stepped on the dead man's hand. In the dim shadows he had not seen him, with his right arm flung out, and his left clamped over his chest, as if to ward off the bullet. Luten froze in his tracks, seized with the black horror that a corpse engenders in us all, that dread realization that we, too, will one day come to this. There was no doubt the man was dead. His half-opened eyes stared unblinkingly at the ceiling. His mouth was agape. The candle tilted in Luten's hand. Melted wax spilled onto his fingers.

Luten straightened the candle and bent down to touch the face. It was cold, clammy. When he tried to lift an arm, it was nearly stiff with rigor mortis. He had been dead for some time, but not more than a few hours, or the oil in the lamp would have been used up. That it had been lit suggested Robinson had been alive after sunset. The bloodstain on his shirt was congealing around the edges.

Luten's instinct was to run from the place, to get as far away from death as he could, as fast as he could.

He had to force himself to remain and look for clues. First a quick look in the man's pockets, where he found a deck of cards and several gentlemen's calling cards—some of them gents of the first stare. He drew out a money purse. It held over fifty pounds. And at the bottom of the money, the stubs of two tickets for the masquerade party at the Pantheon.

He stared at them, his brow furrowed in consternation. Was it possible Corinne was right, that Robinson had been Robin Hood, hired by someone—perhaps paid with this wad of bills in his pocket—to steal the pearls? That, of course, was why he had been murdered. First Rose Grimm, who had supplied the costume, then Robinson, who had stolen the pearls. But who was behind it? He gazed at the inert body and thought of Rosie Grimm, with that stocking around her neck. The murderer had come prepared this time, with his pistol. A well set-up man like Robinson wouldn't be so easily overpowered as Rosie Grimm. Luten felt a murderous rage grow within him. Who dared to take two lives for the mere pleasure of a string of pearls?

The pearls! They might still be here. He had to take himself by the scruff of the neck to search the premises. He rose and began the job. First downstairs, opening every desk and dresser drawer, rummaging behind furniture. Then up the dark box staircase to the living quarters, consisting of a parlor, bedroom and kitchen. The rooms were undisturbed, which suggested that the murderer had got the necklace before killing Robinson. Luten performed a quick search anyway. The only item of the least interest was a woman's green, rather flamboyant night robe in the clothespress. A redhead might very well choose green . . .

He hastened back downstairs. A gust of wind blew the door open. His candle flickered and went out, plunging Luten into blackness. The lamp had burned out while he was abovestairs. He set the candle aside and felt his way past the tables and chairs into the cool night air, where he filled his lungs and breathed a prayer of thanks for the simple fact of being alive. Robinson's death had to be reported to Bow Street. He disliked to do it after reporting Rose Grimm's death the day before. He'd take Townsend into his confidence, tell him the whole story.

As he thought of those two murders, an awful fear for Corinne's safety grew in him. He had to know that she was all right, even if it gave the murderer more time to escape. If anything happened to her ... He urged his driver on to a reckless pace. The carriage rattled through the streets, heedless of the encompassing fog, back to Lady Castlereagh's house.

He arrived to learn from Prance that Corinne had gone off with the Conte de Creuse.

"I've been to Robinson's. He's dead, murdered," Luten said in a hollow voice.

"Good God! You don't suppose de Creuse—he has Corinne!"

"You didn't let her go alone with him!"

"Of course not. She's with Coffen."

"We'll go to his place in my rig. I have it standing by outside. You have the address?"

"Yes, that little cottage Sinclair used to live in when his papa kicked him out."

They said goodnight to Lady Castlereagh and made a discreet departure from the ballroom, damping down the urge to run as fast as their legs could carry them. Luten took the ribbons himself and sent his coachman off to find Prance's driver. The coachmen were to take Prance's rig to Bow Street and report the murder. Prance sat with Luten on the box, hearing an account of Luten's visit to Shepherd's Market.

"Robinson may have stolen the pearls. Those two ticket stubs looks like it," Luten said, "but someone put him up to it. Robinson wouldn't steal anything so valuable. I wager it was put to him as some sort of prank."

"A prank is usually played on one particular person. Don't you think it's beginning to look significant that he wore the same costume as you wore to your own masquerade, and stole Corinne's pearls?"

Luten said grimly, "You mean he was hired to masquerade as me, and steal the pearls? Not just any jewelry, but the pearls. I believe you're right, Prance."

"Is it possible someone is trying to get Corinne into trouble? Several people know she had to return the necklace. And of course every lady in London is jealous of her—especially her rather special relationship with you. Whom have you jilted recently?"

"No jealous lady killed Robinson."

"I wouldn't put this trick past deCoventry—but that makes no sense. He was to get the pearls back legally on Friday. Who else hates her?"

"Corinne doesn't have that sort of enemy," Luten said.

"A pretty lady always has enemies," Prance replied. "But I know what you mean. Her enemies would be jealous cats; these murders look like the work of a man. Though not necessarily. Hell hath no fury . . ."

"Of course it was a man," Luten said sharply. Agitation lent a harsh edge to his words. "It was the *Monsieur* who was seeing Rosie Grimm. Corinne said that Robin Hood didn't have a French accent. She even thought he might have been Robinson, because of his rough hands, but I wouldn't listen to her. If anything's happened to her . . ." He cracked the whip and the team strained forward faster, faster.

"Slow down, Luten. You'll upset the rig," Prance exclaimed, as the wind lifted his hat from his head.

Then they both fell silent. What Prance called the rogue in himself secretly enjoyed the dart through the dark night, with the spice of danger and even tragedy lurking just beneath the anxiety. The moon decided to get in on the act. It revealed its pale face from behind a ragged drift of cloud. Saucy, pedantic wretch. No, that was said of the sun.

They reached the cottage on the banks of the Thames without upsetting the carriage or crippling the team. Luten flung the reins to Prance, leapt down and darted into the house, to see Corinne alone with the *conte*, who was putting his arm around her.

He strode forward and forcibly removed the *conte*'s arm. "Sorry to break up the party, milady, but you are leaving now," he said through gritted teeth. "Where the hell is Coffen? Don't tell me you're here alone!"

Corinne's temper rose at this rough treatment. "Of course not. Not that it's any concern of—" She saw the look of anxious strain on Luten's face, and her heart clenched in fear. "Luten, what's the matter?" she demanded.

"Pray, milord," the *conte* said, smiling tenaciously, "will you not have a glass of wine—"

"Get Mr. Pattle," Luten said in a voice that would raise blisters.

"*Certainement*, milord. It will be my pleasure." The *conte*'s hasty exit had the air of an escape.

Coffen had heard the raised voice and came out, blinking owlishly. "Oh, it's you, Luten."

"We're leaving," Luten said.

"So we are," Coffen said, smiling uncertainly at his host. "A nice party, *conte*." He handed the medals back to another *conte*. "Sorry, not quite my thing." He snatched up his hat. Luten found Corinne's wrap and tossed it over her shoulders.

"Thank you for coming," the Conte de Creuse said. "I hope you will return. Good evening, milady, milord."

He was still thanking them and calling *au revoirs* when the door slammed. He hunched his shoulders at his friends. "Bah, *les anglais*," he said contemptuously. "*Ils sont tous fauves.*"

Luten hustled Corinne toward his carriage, then remembered that he was without a groom. "I have to drive," he said.

She stared as if he had run mad. Glancing to the box, she recognized Prance, who hopped down to embrace her.

"We've suffered agonies, my pet. Tell me you are unharmed."

"Of course I am. Where is John Groom?"

"It's a long story."

Luten took her arm to help her into his rig.

"I'll sit on the box with you," she said.

"Haven't you had enough excitement for one night?" he barked. "I thought it was supposed to be a party you were going to. A party of two is usually called something else."

She turned and stalked off to Coffen's carriage. "Luten is being impossible," she announced and flounced in.

"Tahrsome feller. I thought he was in a bit of a pelter. Some trouble with his coachman?" Coffen asked.

She tossed her head and replied, "I haven't the faintest idea. Will you please take me home, Coffen?"

"I'll just have a word with Luten first," Coffen said, and went to the other carriage.

"My place," Luten called down.

Prance jumped up beside him just as he sprang the horses. "I say, Luten. No need to take it out on Corinne," he said.

Luten knew it very well, but he had been in such anxiety that when he saw her, with that damned Frenchie putting his hands on her, he lost his head. What had begun as a simple robbery had grown into a double murder. It was some deep plot against himself and Corinne, or why had Robinson been given that particular costume to wear? Why had the theft occurred at his masquerade party? Why had the pearls been stolen just days before they were to be turned over to deCoventry? His life had not been blameless. He had accumulated his share of enemies, particularly in the House, where he was a thorn in the side of Mouldy and Company. But why drag Corinne into it? Was someone trying to make her believe *he* had stolen the pearl necklace?

Corinne was torn between going home in a huff and curiosity to learn what had put Luten in such a pelter. Curiosity won out. When Coffen's carriage drew up in front of Luten's house, she got out and went inside. Luten and Prance had already arrived. She knew as soon as she entered that Luten had recovered from his fit of pique. He didn't apologize, but he wore his apologetic face.

"Now perhaps you will tell me what is going on," she said.

It was Prance who answered. "Robinson has been murdered."

Corinne felt her legs turn to water. She sagged against Coffen, who assisted her to a chair. "You didn't have to shout it at her," Coffen said. "It ain't her fault."

Prance fell to his knees in front of her and seized her two hands in his. "Forgive me, my dear. It was savage of me to fling the thing at you so suddenly. But you know I never can quite control my love of dramatics."

"But is it true?" Corinne asked.

"Indeed it is. Unless Luten has told me a Banbury tale, and I cannot see the point of that." He looked a question at Luten. "No, I acquit him of such a brutality. I have never seen him so distraught, except perhaps the time he lost that race to Yarrow. There was five hundred pounds riding on it."

"For God's sake, shut up, Prance," Luten said. "It's true, Corinne. Robinson's dead." He paced the room, with one hand massaging his forehead.

"Let us have wine before we hear the story," Prance suggested. "Corinne is pale as a ghost. I feel undone myself."

He poured wine and they all settled in, first to hear the tale, then to discuss its ramifications.

Chapter Twelve

Luten's elegant Gold Saloon with its silk brocade window hangings, its weighty gilt-framed mirrors and paintings, its priceless carpets and Chippendale furnishings was an unlikely place to discuss murder. It was designed for more gracious goings-on: for serving tea to dowager aunts, for entertaining royal dukes or for planning strategies against Mouldy and Company, but not for murder.

Luten outlined the story, curtailing the description of how he had found Robinson for Corinne's sake. "He had been shot some time before," was all he said, but he would never forget the awful sight of those staring eyes, and gaping mouth. "I believe you were right, Corinne. The tickets to the Pantheon suggest he was Robin Hood, but I doubt he murdered Rose Grimm. He was no 'fine gent.' "

They discussed why he had worn this disguise, if not to pass for Luten, and more important, who had put him up to it.

"Seems to me," Coffen said, rubbing his ear, "we'll never know who was behind it all now. Rosie got him the suit—she's dead. Robinson wore it and stole the pearls—he's dead. Who's left to quiz?"

Corinne said, "We must find the redheaded lady."

"How?" Coffen asked. There was no answer.

"I'll go back to Drury Lane tomorrow and try to discover whether Rose told anyone the name of the man she was seeing," Luten said, "but I fear it's useless. Even if she had told anyone, the man wouldn't have given her his own name."

"Perhaps he didn't even give her his true nationality," Prance suggested. "I refer, of course, to her calling him *Monsieur*. That could be a clever diversion."

"I'm sure the French émigrés we met tonight have nothing to do with it," Corinne said. "They're just poor disinherited boys trying to make a living. If this was a personal grudge against me—or you, Luten—then it wasn't a Frenchman. We don't know any of them well enough to have caused a grudge."

Luten nodded. "As Coffen said, we've run dry attacking it from this end. We must try it from another angle. Why were the pearls, and nothing else, stolen at the masquerade? The Pantheon was glittering with gems, some of them more valuable than the pearls. Diamonds would be easier to sell. The piece can be broken up and the gems sold separately. The pearls are unique. Their value rests in their being perfectly matched. To break them up and sell them separately would decimate their value."

"And they couldn't be worn in public without being recognized," Prance added.

"Precisely," Luten said impatiently, and continued his speech. "A man of my build dressed as Robin Hood, presumably Robinson, threw himself in Corinne's path the moment she arrived at the party. Who knows I dressed as Robin Hood last autumn at my own masquerade ball?"

"Half the town," Coffen said. "You had three hundred guests. A regular crush."

"We won't get far following that tack," Luten agreed. "What we must discover is who wanted those pearls badly enough to kill two people to get them."

"I expect you're thinking of deCoventry," Corinne said, "but as I was to give them to him in a few days' time, he didn't have to steal or murder to get them."

"She's right," Prance said, frowning into the grate. "Could it be one of those queer nabs who likes to hoard up beautiful things in a dark room where no one but himself can enjoy them? When something so unique and beautiful as that necklace is stolen, one does wonder."

"I don't see it as the work of a lunatic," Luten said. "It was too well organized, too thoroughly executed."

"Your wits are gone begging," Coffen said, looking around with a satisfied smile on his pink face. "The pearls couldn't be worn in London, but when you call them unique, they ain't the Mona Lisa, or St. Paul's Cathedral."

"What are you getting at, if anything, Coffen?" Prance demanded. "I've never heard of anyone wearing a painting as a necklace. As to Saint Paul's—it would take a giant to carry it. A Gulliver in the land of Lilliputians."

Coffen replied suavely, "What I mean is that the pearls could be worn in some place other than London without being recognized. They ain't *that* famous. Rose Grimm's lad spoke French. The pearls are likely even now on a lugger to France."

Prance looked quite startled. "I do apologize, Pattle. I believe you have accidentally hit on something here."

"It wasn't accidental," Coffen replied, unoffended. "I put my mind to it. I do that sometimes."

"You're suggesting that it was not someone with a grudge against myself or Luten who stole them, but just a French thief?" Corinne asked.

"You've got it now." Coffen nodded. "A French pearl lover. And don't bother telling me that you don't know any Frenchies, for one meets them everywhere. You've worn those pearls to Castlereagh's before tonight. Their saloon is full of foreigners. Likely that's where the Frenchies spotted them."

After a frowning pause, Luten said, "It still seems more logical to steal something that could be worn or sold without taking it to France." He turned to Corinne. "Does the necklace have any historical associations? Did it, by any chance, come from France—perhaps in a questionable manner? I'm thinking of something along the lines of the Blue Tavernier diamond that was stolen during the revolution when the French crown jewels were put on public display."

"No, George's nabob uncle brought it home from India. It's never been to France, to the best of my knowledge."

"Like me," Prance said, and sighed. "One never feels really civilized until he's seen Paree."

"It's there now. Depend upon it," Coffen said. Having solved the matter, he rose, made his bows and left. He was hungry, and there was obviously to be no snack forthcoming.

"It is rather late," Prance said, rising. He turned to Corinne. "I'll accompany you across the street, my dear."

"Did you report Robinson's death, Luten?" Corinne asked.

"My coachman was to report it to Bow Street," he replied.

Prance said, "I have no doubt Bow Street will arrive here in my carriage with John Groom e'er long to quiz us. That will cause quite a stir in the neighborhood. Let me get you home, my pet. I want to spare you the grisly details. I know I shan't sleep a wink after the coming interview. I shall have my esteemed André add a tea-spoon of brandy to my posset tonight. I suggest you have Mrs. Ballard do the same."

Corinne looked to Luten, thinking he might offer to walk home with her. But his mind was on the coming interview with Bow Street. He just accompanied them to the door and watched as Prance led her off. Prance, being perfectly aware of it, dallied on her doorstep. Before letting her go, he placed a kiss on her cheek.

"That will give Luten something to think about," he said, mischievously. "And me too." Then he kissed her again and left.

Corinne did indeed have trouble sleeping. The awful events of the past twenty-four hours spun in her head. The theft of the pearls that did not belong to her and had to be returned in three days. Why had she worn them, and to the Pantheon, of all places? She thought of the two murders. Mostly of Rose, since she had not actually seen Robinson's face. She racked her brain for some excuse to delay handing the necklace over to deCoventry. She felt she could bring him around her thumb, but Lady deCoventry was another matter. At the first sign of reluctance, she would start crying for a lawyer.

Her mind also kept harping on the redheaded woman. She had been right that the man who stole the pearls was not a Frenchman, but no one listened to her until they had discovered it for themselves. They discounted the redhead's importance because she was a woman, but if she was Robinson's accomplice, as Luten thought, then she knew what lay behind this theft. When she learned that Robinson had been killed, she might be frightened into talking. Robinson might even have given her the pearls for safekeeping. How could she be found? A carefully worded advertisement in the journals? It was worth a try. She'd send one in tomorrow.

After her fretful night, she rose late in the morning. As soon as she went downstairs, she peered out the front window at the elegant façade of Luten's house, wondering if he was up and about yet. As she watched, Scamp drove his shining yellow curricle up to the house. Luten came out and hopped into it. He glanced at her house. She hurried to the front door, but he had already driven off by the time she got the door open. Perhaps he was going to Drury Lane. She prayed he would discover something to help her.

It was Luten whom she expected to be shown in when the door knocker sounded an hour later. She had spent the interval composing her notice for the journals. But when Black appeared at her saloon, he said, "Mr. Smythe to see you, your ladyship."

"Who is he? What does he want?" she asked.

"It's about insurance, milady."

"Tell him I'm out."

The butler cleared his throat discreetly. Luten's butler

had told him a mighty interesting tale this morning, when he slipped across the street to discover what Bow Street had been doing there in the middle of the night. The Berkeley Brigade were in hot water this time for certain.

"It's about the pearls, your ladyship," he said, with a sapient nod.

Her hopes soared, collided with confusion, and fell to earth. She had heard of thieves selling purloined items back to the insurance company for a fraction of their value, but the pearls were not insured, so Mr. Smythe could not have them.

"You had best send him in. And Black, will you send a footman across the road to see if Lord Luten has come back yet?"

"I'll ask him to come the minute he arrives."

"You're invaluable, Black."

He bowed his head graciously and retreated, holding to his heart the smile she had bestowed on him. He felt his first duty was to linger at the saloon doorway to listen to what was said after showing Smythe in, and called for a footman to stand on guard at the front door for Luten's arrival.

Mr. Smythe was an inoffensive clerk with thinning hair, a long face and a badly cut jacket. He entered uncertainly, ill at ease to be confronting a countess.

"I am here on Lord deCoventry's behalf, your ladyship," he explained. "It is about the deCoventry pearls."

Her throat went dry. "What—what about them?" she asked in a quavering voice.

"His lordship has decided to have all the family jewels insured. A wise precaution, if I may say so. Of course they must first be authenticated. The other pieces have been assessed by a reputable jeweler. Only the pearls remain to be examined. His lordship wondered if you would let them be examined today, to facilitate the writing of the policy for the entire collection. It would take only an hour. You would have them back this afternoon."

Corinne sat like a stone. She had been planning what

she would say to deCoventry when the dreaded time came to hand them over, but she had not expected this. She was so distraught she did not hear Luten coming in at the front door. He had seen the ramshackle gig in front of Corinne's house. Fearing an attempt was being made to sell her back the pearls, he went dashing across the road to lend his assistance even before the footman hailed him.

Black darted to the door to greet him. He put his fingers to his lips and said, "DeCoventry has sent an insurance cove over for the pearls. Says he wants to insure all his sparklers. Sounds havey-cavey to me."

Luten blinked once in astonishment. "Thank you, Black," he said. "You need not announce me just yet." He edged silently along the wall to listen to what was being said in the saloon.

He heard Corinne say, in a voice several degrees higher than her usual cellolike tones, "Actually, they're not in the house at the moment." Mr. Smythe smiled on, unsuspecting. His demeanor gave her courage. "I took them to Love and Wirgams to have them cleaned, the clasp checked and so on, before returning them to Lord deCoventry," she explained.

"I'll run down to Love and Wirgams now. They are more than reputable. The jeweler there can authenticate the piece, and I can proceed with writing up the policy."

Invention failed her. She was about to crop out into a confession when Black appeared at the doorway. "Your ladyship. I am sorry to interrupt, but Lord Luten would like a word. Most urgently," he added.

Relief flooded through her. "If you will excuse me, Mr. Smythe," she said, and followed Black out. She had to force herself to maintain a ladylike gait.

She saw Luten hiding just beyond the door. "You heard?" she asked, panic edging her words.

"Stall him. I'll run down to Love and Wirgams and tell them to refuse to show him the pearls."

"Oh, thank you, dear Luten!" she exclaimed.

Luten had thought her gratitude might take a more physical turn, but she didn't kiss him. She just held his fingers a moment, with her eyes shining.

A much relieved Lady deCoventry returned to the saloon. "Now where were we, Mr. Smythe? Ah yes, you were saying that Love and Wirgams will authenticate the pearls."

"I will require written permission from yourself to gain access to them," he said apologetically.

"Of course. I shan't be a moment."

She left at a stately pace, told Black to give Mr. Smythe a glass of sherry, and went to the study to write the statement Smythe required. She had complete reliance on Luten's ingenuity and toplofty way. He would arrange it that the jeweler did not betray that he didn't have the pearls. She didn't know how Luten would accomplish it, but she knew he would. Her fingers were trembling so badly she spoiled two sheets of her crested writing paper. She took as long as she dared to write up the permission, to give Luten time to coerce the jewelers. Then she took the note to Mr. Smythe, who thanked her effusively and left.

She sat on alone in the saloon for forty-five minutes, worrying. Why was deCoventry in such a rush to insure the estate jewelry? Did he know she had lost the pearls? How could he—unless he was involved himself? But Prance had said the word would be around town by now, due to their investigations. Oh why didn't Luten come?

Chapter Thirteen

"I would like to speak to the manager, at once," Luten announced to the clerk, when he entered the jewelry shop.

"Certainly, milord. Step this way."

Luten followed the clerk past rows of glass-fronted cases displaying watches, rings and brooches to an office at the rear of the shop. The room was paneled in oak, and rigged out like a gentleman's study. Luten adopted his most arrogant expression and said, "I am the Marquess of Luten, here on behalf of Lady deCoventry. There's a fellow running around town, claiming to be an insurance tout, asking the jewelers if they have the deCoventry pearls."

Pennyworth, a sharp-eyed merchant wearing a diamond on his small finger and another in his cravat, rose from behind his desk and bowed. "Delighted to make your acquaintance, milord. As to the pearls you mention, however, I don't have them."

"I am aware of that, Mr. Pennyworth. I assume you would not be foolhardy enough to display valuable jewels in your safekeeping to any hedgebird who comes in off the street with a forged document, calling himself an insurance agent. What I object to is telling these men anything at all. I trust it is not your policy to do so?"

"Oh certainly not, milord," Pennyworth lied.

"Excellent. Then I can count on you to tell this man—he calls himself Smythe—nothing at all."

"I shall refuse to speak to him!"

"Very proper. You might have a word with your clerks to see they don't reveal the whereabouts of the necklace."

"I will, milord," Pennyworth said, although he had no idea where the necklace was.

"Thank you. I commend your discretion."

Pennyworth shifted uncomfortably in his seat. "About the deCoventry pearls, there is a rumor afoot that they have been stolen already?" His voice made it a question. "I was told by my staff that you, yourself, were here making enquiries . . ."

Luten's eyebrows rose toward his hairline. "Stolen? Where do these rumors come from? It is true Lady deCoventry misplaced them. The clasp came loose and they fell off the other night. In a panic, she asked me to handle it for her, to tell the jewelry shops to notify me at once if anyone tried to sell them. They were recovered the same day in the clothes basket. I fear these rumors have alerted the thieving crew to the value of the necklace, which is why we must be particularly careful just now."

"Why would a thief think they're here?" Pennyworth asked.

"They're making enquiries at all the better jewelry shops," Luten said, throwing in a compliment to make his unlikely story go down more smoothly. "Naturally her ladyship would have them repaired when she broke the clasp. The intention, obviously, is to discover which shop she took them to, break into the shop and steal them. Lady deCoventry had a jeweler come to her house to do the job, as she was afraid of letting them out of her hands."

"Very wise. Should the need arise again, I have a lad who would be happy to go to her house."

"I shall be sure to tell her so." Having gained his end, he settled in for a few friendly words. "I expect you do work for the *legitimate* insurance trade, from time to time?"

"We have to oblige our better customers, but we steer

clear of it as much as possible. We have had cases where a lady has us evaluate the authentic piece, then runs off and has a copy made elsewhere. She wears the copy to a ball and arranges to have it stolen in front of witnesses, then uses our expertise to assure the insurance company that the genuine article was in her possession at the time of the robbery. Oh, they are up to all the rigs! And there are such excellent copies nowadays, too, that you can't tell the difference. The techniques are improving every day. A bit of foil leaf behind a piece of faceted glass makes a dandy diamond.

"As to pearls! There's a jeweler on the continent who has found a way to add a mild abrasive to a fishpaste bead, giving it a very good lustre and texture. A real pearl has a gentle roughness to it. Unless you scratched away the skin of the fake pearl and saw the glass bead beneath, no one but an expert would ever know the difference. They lack the lustre of a genuine pearl. Seen against a white paper an expert would know a fake to see it. The lustre cannot so easily be duplicated. Of course much depends on the setting," he continued, and spoke on for a few minutes.

To escape, Luten said, "I noticed some interesting cravat pins on my way in. I shall have a look at them before leaving."

Pennyworth rose and led Luten into the shop. Then he went from clerk to clerk, whispering in each ear, while Luten dawdled over the tray of cravat pins, his hand raised to shield his face, while awaiting Smythe's arrival.

Mr. Smythe received short shrift when he entered the shop ten minutes later. "But I am with Lloyd's Insurance Company!" he said, when he was refused any information.

"So you say," the clerk told him, with a dismissing look.

"I have a letter here from Lady deCoventry giving permission," Smythe insisted, drawing out the letter.

"Paper is cheap. If her ladyship wants her pearls

authenticated, she'll call us to her house. Now run along, lad, before I call Bow Street. I have work to do."

As Smythe left the shop, the clerk turned to Luten. "Milord," he said, fawning a smile at him. "Here is a lovely bit of diamond. Five carats."

Luten felt obliged to buy something, but five carats was overdoing it. "Gaudy!" he said dismissingly. He left shortly, with a new gold horseshoe watchfob in his pocket, and a promise that he would think about a cravat pin. He drove straight to Berkeley Square, where Corinne was so impatient for his return that she answered the door herself.

"What happened?" she demanded, as soon as he stepped in.

"Where's Black?" he asked. "It is unseemly for you to be answering your own door, Countess."

This was not the time for a squabble. She led Luten into the saloon and repeated her question.

"I managed to bring Smythe to a standstill at the jewelry shop," he told her. "That buys us a few days."

"Unless deCoventry comes in person and asks me to let the jeweler examine the necklace. What could I tell him? And why is he in such a rush to have it insured? Do you think he's heard the necklace is stolen, and is trying to force me to tell him?"

"He may have heard a rumor; he has no proof. I managed to satisfy Pennyworth's curiosity. Let us hope he spreads the word the pearls are safe in your possession."

"That was kind of you, Luten. I am in your debt."

"I went to Drury Lane first thing this morning. I could learn nothing. Phoebe assures me that Rose was seeing a gent of the first stare. Rose was coy about it, but she did say more than once that the French were very romantic."

"Most gentlemen speak some French, or can do an accent at least. Rose would be easy to fool, I should think."

"It could be a diversion, as Prance said."

They had run out of ideas. Corinne showed Luten the

notice she had written up for the journals, asking the red-headed lady who accompanied Mr. R. to the Pantheon charity masquerade to be in touch with Lady deC., on Berkeley Square.

"Don't use your own name or address. Use a journal box number," was Luten's only comment.

"Who are we trying to fool? The thief and murderer knows that I'm involved. I don't mention the pearls, you see, so deCoventry will not twig to it."

"If the redhead knows enough to be of any help, she knows who you are. She hasn't come forward. She's either in on it—the most logical thing—or willing to keep silent."

"If she's in on it, she might have the necklace. I'd like to buy it back."

"The murderer has got it. If he hadn't got it from Robinson, the shop would have been pulled apart looking for it. It wasn't. Scratch that Lady deC. No need to tell the rest of the world that you're in a pickle. I wouldn't count on much coming of this, Corinne."

"Well, I shall leave out the Lady deC., and just say 'the lady from Berkeley Square.' "

"Ask her to contact me, if you like."

Corinne didn't reply. She was grateful to Luten, but he was a great one for taking over. She wanted to receive the letter or visit herself, if there was a reply to her notice. And she didn't plan to hold up proceedings by using a box number either. She called for coffee, and they sat, worrying together.

"There isn't even time to get a fake set of pearls made up to give deCoventry, just to stall him," she said. "The pearls would be available. The clasp would be more difficult."

"Pity. Pennyworth—he's the man I spoke to at Love and Wirgams—tells me they can make an excellent fake pearl nowadays. But not good enough to fool an expert, and deCoventry plans to take them to an expert. I wonder if this insurance business isn't just an excuse to authenticate them." He sat, deep in thought, with a frown growing between his eyebrows. Then he looked up and said, "Are you certain the pearls you wore *were* genuine? A forgery couldn't be made in a day or two, but with time, it could be done."

"Of course I'm sure. George would have known if they were fake. I wore them just a week before he died."

"But you retired to Appleby Court for a year after George's death. Did you take the necklace with you?"

"No, I left it in the safe. I knew I wouldn't be going out during my mourning period."

There was a moment's uncomfortable silence as they both remembered the affair at Appleby Court, when Luten had offered for her.

At length, he said, "And Harry stayed here, to look after the house." He directed a meaningful look at her.

"Are you suggesting Harry had a copy made and sold the original?" She felt as if she'd been kicked in the stomach.

"And who would he sell them to?" she asked.

"Stop Hole Abbey, for a tenth of their worth. They'd refashion the pearls into two smaller necklaces or some such thing. It would explain why the pearls were the only thing stolen at the masquerade. He knew his papa was going to have them insured, that they'd be subjected to an examination. He stole the copy so no one would find out he'd taken the original. He was at my masquerade party last fall, so he would know about my Robin Hood costume."

"Everyone knows about that! And he wasn't at the Pantheon. He was home with his mama."

"He made a point of telling you that, did he? He didn't have to be at the Pantheon. In fact, he'd likely find an excuse not to be. He hired Robinson to steal the necklace for him. Robinson would know he was your—what is he exactly?"

"My nephew-in-law, and friend," she said sadly.

"I wager Harry convinced Robinson it was a little prank."

"Harry was at Lady Castlereagh's ball last night. He couldn't have killed Robinson."

Luten noticed her eagerness to protect Harry, and was annoyed. "Robinson had been dead for hours before I found him. Harry fits Baxter's description of Rose Grimm's beau."

"No, I can't believe it."

"I know you're fond of Harry, Corinne, but I think we must look into this further," he said stiffly. "Baxter may be able to identify the man who visited Rose the night she was murdered."

"It wasn't Harry. I'm sure of it."

"Then you don't object to letting Baxter take a look at him without Harry's knowledge."

"You mean set a trap for Harry? Invite him here and have Baxter hiding. That's horrid. I can't do this to him."

"Are you forgetting two people have been brutally murdered?" he asked sharply. "Who is to say that is the end of the slaughter? There may be others involved. The redheaded woman, for instance. And if I'm right, someone made the copy of the pearls. Do you think *he'll* be allowed to live, when the other witnesses have all been killed?"

She shook her head, as if trying to shake away the facts. "I'm sure Harry wouldn't—" Then she stopped. But Harry was desperate for money. He had already stolen from her. His own family hadn't a good word to say of him. He'd had access to her house unhindered for a year.

"The pearls were locked in the safe while I was gone," she said. "The safe hadn't been tampered with when I came back. It has a stout padlock."

"Did you take the key with you?"

"No. But I had it well hidden. There's a secret compartment at the back of the top drawer in George's dresser."

"Harry had twelve months in which to discover it—or pick the lock, or even have a locksmith in to make a key. He's probably murdered him, too. Why do you think he was so eager to stay here that year?"

"He wasn't getting along with his papa. It was convenient for me to have him here. The house was being redecorated. I invited him; he didn't ask me if he could come."

"I expect he dropped some broad hints."

He had, but Corinne was reluctant to admit it. She thought back to that period of turmoil at the time of her husband's death and her remove from deCoventry House to this smaller mansion on Berkeley Square. It had needed a deal of work. Harry had called often, and tried to divert her. It had been Harry's suggestion that she have the house redone while she was at Appleby Court.

"I wouldn't like to have the workmen here while I'm away," she had said. "Lady Sefton did that, and when she came back, her dining room had been painted bright yellow. She wanted it in butter yellow. It looked horrid."

"You'd want someone with a good eye in his head to keep a watch on things," Harry had said, or something like that.

And then she had asked him if he was interested.

"It might have been some of Harry's friends," she said, grasping at straws. "His friends called on him here. Some of Harry's friends are no better than they should be."

"Birds of a feather . . . Did this imaginary friend also discover the key in the secret compartment at the back of George's dresser? You're refusing to face facts, Corinne. How would a friend know that deCoventry plans to have the jewelry assessed at this particular time? You didn't know it yourself until Smythe's call. But Harry would know."

"He isn't like that, Luten," she said helplessly. "Even if he took the pearls, he would never kill anyone. He'd hop on a ship to India, but he wouldn't kill a woman in cold blood."

"There's no saying what a man will do when he's faced with the gibbet."

"It wouldn't come to that! DeCoventry would help him."

"Well, faced with disgrace, in any case. With the humiliation of his family, those he cares for most deeply, knowing he was a thief."

She thought about it for a moment. "I think Harry would just confess and throw himself on our mercy," she said, remembering the episode of the Meissen box. Her eyes turned to it. She could see, in her mind's eye, Harry peering furtively over his shoulder, taking the box from the table, secreting it in his pocket, then brazenly asking her if she could loan him a few bob. Cool as a cucumber he'd been. Perhaps she didn't know Harry as well as she thought she did. She became aware that Luten was speaking again, and shook herself back to attention.

"If you're so certain of his innocence, then let Baxter take a look at him. That will settle it, one way or the other."

She couldn't go on living with the uncertainty, wondering every time Harry called if he was a thief, and a murderer.

"Yes, you're right," she said. "How shall we arrange it?"

"Invite Harry to dinner tonight."

"No! If we must lay a trap, I would prefer not to do it under my own roof. I feel a very Judas."

"How would you feel if he murders someone else?"

She didn't answer, but just sat, staring into space, so distraught that Luten regretted his bluntness.

"I have a box at Covent Garden. I shall invite him to join me this evening," she said in a dull voice.

"Fine. You drop Harry a note. I'll wait until I hear he's accepted before visiting Baxter. Meanwhile I have something else I want to look into."

He knew when Corinne didn't ask any questions that she was in some private purgatory. He had always known she was fond of Harry. It was beginning to look as if she were more than fond of him. As far as Luten was concerned, the case was solved. DeCoventry wouldn't raise a fuss when he learned his own son had stolen the necklace—nor, obviously, would Corinne. It would be swept under the carpet, and Harry would walk free. But there were still two murders to be accounted for.

He was no more eager for the evening to unfold than she was, but the thing must be done. Meanwhile, he would try to discover who had made the forged necklace for Harry, if indeed there *was* a forged necklace, and warn him to be on guard for his life. He'd ask Pennyworth for the name of London's premier maker of false pearls. Whoever had made the copy must be good. Corinne had worn the pearls several times since her return from Appleby Court, and neither she nor himself nor anyone else had detected a forgery.

He left, with an ominous feeling that he might already be too late. Harry was covering his traces well.

Chapter Fourteen

At eleven o'clock in the morning, Sir Reginald Prance put the finishing touches to his toilette and preened a moment in front of the mirror before leaving his toilet table. He followed Beau Brummell's dictum that a gentleman should prepare himself with sufficient care before leaving his room that he was set for the day. To be yanking at a cravat or pulling down an ill-fitting jacket was the mark of a Johnnie Raw.

Prance's jacket of blue superfine, made by London's premier tailor, Weston, was drawn neat as a second skin over his shoulders. He spurned the brass buttons that might be seen anywhere for a set of nacre ones with just a delicate hint of opaline flush on their polished surface. His waistcoat took up the hints of pinkish-purple in narrow stripes. His shirt points were fashionably high without approaching the ludicrous. As to his boots! You could see your face in them. And the secret was not champagne, as Beau had said, surely in jest. Every valet in town had tried it, resulting in a week of extremely untidy boots. No sir, the secret was plain old Kelly's bootblack and plenty of his valet's elbow-grease.

When there was nothing further that art could add to nature, Prance descended to his morning parlor, where he found the most rumpled, inelegant gentleman in London having a second breakfast, when he really ought to forgo even one if he ever hoped to achieve an elegant silhouette.

"Good day, Pattle," he said, lifting the lids of the hot

dishes on the sideboard and sniffing. Could he manage a nibble of kipper this morning? No, adamantly no. He lifted two fingers of toast to his plate with the tongs and sat down. "To what do I owe the honor, et cetera?"

Coffen looked up from the plate. A dribble of butter ran down his chin. "Eh? If you mean why am I here, it's because of helping Corinne, of course."

"Wipe your chin. Not with your fingers!" he said crossly, as Coffen brushed the butter away with his hand.

"I didn't want to dirty your nice napkin."

"That is the purpose of a napkin, Pattle."

Coffen daubed at his chin with the napkin, examined it, frowned and said, "I called on Luten. He was out. I thought you and I might have a word with Corinne."

Prance was always happy to make up to Corinne behind Luten's back. "Excellent," he said, and applied his knife and fork to a piece of toast, while Coffen looked on, shaking his head at such finicking behavior and rubbing his greasy fingers against the legs of his trousers.

Two toast fingers later, they were just leaving the house as Luten came out of Corinne's front door. They hailed him to discover what was afoot.

As Luten was driving his carriage, they all piled in for the trip to Love and Wirgams. Luten filled them in on Smythe's visit, his own first visit to the jeweler and his belief that Harry was the culprit.

"It's possible," Prance said, "though if the deCoventrys are involved, Harry would be my last choice. He hasn't the nous for such deep thinking. Gaviston—"

"He's thick as a plank," Luten said dismissingly. "The reason Castlereagh holds him in such high esteem is because he has an excellent memory, and parrots everything Castlereagh says."

"True. His head is solid oak. Old deCoventry, then. The connection to Drury Lane is there in Esmee, and he don't limit his flirts to one. He might have had a liaison with Rose."

Coffen shook his head. "More likely he'd have a girl

110

from Covent Garden, if he had a second one, I mean. Esmee is a Tartar. She'd have heard about Rose, and given him what for. Harry is the likeliest one to have been carrying on with Rose. He couldn't afford a high flyer like Esmee, but why try to involve Luten at all?"

"A mystery shrouded in an enigma," Prance declared, "unless, perhaps, to turn Corinne against Luten, to clear the path for himself."

Luten was glad someone else had said what he thought himself. "That is entirely possible. He's always hanging out for an heiress."

"Corinne goes along with your notion, does she?" Coffen asked. "Mean to say, she's fond of Harry. I like him myself, come to that. As he was living in Corinne's house for a year, you may be sure his papa and Gaviston—and even his mama—called on him. Any of them might have done it."

Prance listened closely. "You don't suppose the old lady . . . she's been green with jealousy of Corinne ever since George married her. Afraid she'd produce an heir as well. Then to have to share the title of Lady deCoventry with a young Incomparable! Really one can understand her ill humor."

"She could hardly pass herself off as a French gentleman," Luten said. "Rose was not well educated, but one assumes she could tell an old lady from a young gentleman."

"There is that," Prance conceded. "Mind you, Lady deCoventry's lads would do anything for her. She might have put Harry up to it. If she could get Corinne accused of being a thief, it would remove a most painful thorn from her side."

"The old girl is religious," Luten reminded him.

"Yes, such loud rectitude must hide a dark core, though, don't you think? 'Some soul of goodness in thy evil,' Shakespeare says. It stands to reason there is equally some evil in an excess of goodness. I know I always feel a strong urge to sin when the Reformers preach at me. An instinctive search for balance, I expect."

"I know what you mean," Coffen said. "I want to eat with my hands when I see you hacking at your toast with a knife and fork. Anyhow, if it's balance you're after, you've got the good and the bad in the deCoventrys. Dash it, it's beginning to look like a family plot."

"I don't see that Harry required any help," Luten countered.

They arrived at the jewelry shop. "You do the questioning, Prance," Luten said. "The clerk will try to sell me a diamond. Speak to Pennyworth. He's the one who knows the local forgers."

Prance liked jewelry shops. He could hardly tear himself away from the display cases, but eventually he spoke to Pennyworth and returned to report to Luten.

"Definitely suspicious," he announced. "Pennyworth spoke of a new process for making forged pearls."

"I know all about that," Luten said. "Did you get a name?"

"A Mr. Gregory, on Poland Street, was the only man in London who had tried this new process, and it seems even he was not entirely successful."

"Was?" Luten barked the word. "You mean—"

"Killed in his shop six months ago. It was reported as murder as a result of a robbery. The jewelry he was working on was all stolen. Some of it was picked up later at Stop Hole Abbey. Looks like a professional job. Bow Street held a certain Lefty Muldoon responsible. He hung for it, swearing his innocence. Of course they always do."

"By God, I was right!" Luten said grimly. "Harry did have the pearls copied, and killed Gregory to conceal it."

"With such a complete hand at the helm, it occurs to me we ought to make sure Baxter is still alive," Prance said. "If he is removed as well, we're left witnessless."

"You mean witless," Coffen informed him. "The word's witless, Reg."

"In your case, certainly."

A look of alarm seized Luten's face. "I'm going to take Baxter home with me," he said, and had the team whipped up to drive to Stukeley Street.

They found Baxter repairing the doorknob of the ramshackle apartment house. His eyes were red, from lack of sleep or perhaps from gin. He proved unbiddable.

"I'll not stir from home," he said. "I'm close to the theater. I keep an eye on comings and goings. One day I'll see him, and when I do!" His meaty hands clenched into fists.

"You might see him tonight," Luten said. Baxter's red eyes bulged in eagerness. "I'm working on something. I'll be back to give you the details, and for God's sake, man, be careful of yourself."

"I'll not stick my fork in the wall till I get the bastard that kilt my Rosie. What do you have in mind, then?"

Luten outlined his plan, omitting Harry's name, in case Baxter decided to take matters into his own hands. Baxter expressed every eagerness to identify the man in question.

"Do you have a gun?" Luten asked him, before leaving.

Baxter pulled a sharp knife out of his waistband. A blade six inches long glinted in the dim light. "I don't need a gun," he said, with a menacing grin.

Prance winced and turned away. Coffen's Adam's apple bobbed up and down. As the three drove to Berkeley Square, Prance said, "I've been thinking—it was unwise to call on Baxter. Until now, the murderer hasn't realized he was seen. If he's keeping an eye on us, he might wonder why we visited Baxter. With this epidemic of murders . . ."

Luten swore off a string of curses. "You're right, damn your eyes. Well, we can't go back and warn him. That would only compound the folly." He put his head out the window and peered behind to make sure they were not being followed.

"Hire Rosie's room," Coffen said. "It's empty. Put a footman in it, in disguise, to keep an eye on Baxter."

Prance smiled blandly. "You never cease to amaze, Pattle. That is three ideas you've had in as many days."

"I have them all the time. Nobody listens to me."

No one was listening to him again. Luten was busy deciding which of his servants was the wiliest. He settled on his second groom, Willie Watson. They returned to Berkeley Square to discuss with Willie what identity he would use when he hired a room on Stukeley Street. Prance's suggestion that he pose as a highwayman lying low after a job found favor. It would account for Willie's staying close to the house.

While this was going forth, Corinne had a footman deliver her invitation to Lord Harry, and her appeal to the redheaded lady to the three major journals. When a caller was announced not thirty minutes later, she had the absurd notion her advertisement was being answered, but it was Lord Gaviston who was shown in. Her heart jumped into her throat. He had learned that the pearls were missing! What could she do?

When he appeared at the door, wearing his usual amiable smile, her fears subsided to curiosity.

"Good morning, Gaviston," she said. "This is an unexpected pleasure. I thought you'd be at work at this hour."

"Just on my way. I'm here on Harry's behalf, actually. Your invitation to the theater arrived as I was leaving. He's sent his reply with me as he was having breakfast. He is delighted to accept. He didn't write to thank you, I fear. That's Harry all over." He leaned forward and continued in a confidential tone, "*Entre nous*, Corinne, I'm delighted you're taking an interest in the lad. He's running with a pretty raffish set lately. Lady Angela doesn't like it."

Corinne wondered at this curious addendum. "I'm sure we are all sorry to hear it," she said. "Perhaps you and Lady Angela could steer him into better company."

Gaviston smiled his foolish smile, but there was a

glitter of slyness in his eyes. "There is no company he prefers to yours. A good wife would be the making of him."

Corinne soon figured out that Lady deCoventry had put Gaviston up to this stunt. She said firmly, "Harry and I are good friends. There's never been more than that between us."

"If it's the fact that he was George's nevvie—well, he's actually no blood kin to you. One could always get a dispensation. I know a bishop—"

"It's not that."

"A lady could do worse. He's a handsome devil, and cheerful. Always a joke and a smile. I don't know how he does it. Of course he has not my concerns to keep him awake nights. He doesn't realize the wretched condition of three quarters of the population of London. But we shan't go into that. Well, and how are you keeping yourself these days?" He examined her closely. "Enjoying the season, are you?"

"Very much."

"You left Castlereagh's early last night, leaving a good many disappointed gentlemen behind. They were all asking what the Berkeley Brigade was up to, tearing off *en masse*, first from Luten's masquerade ball, then Lady Castlereagh's do." He peered at her curiously.

"We went on to another party," she said vaguely.

"Surely not with that French fellow you were standing up with? The so-called Conte de Creuse."

"With Coffen Pattle, actually," she replied.

"The reason I thought it might be the *conte*, he and his crew all disappeared at the same time as yourself. And of course you did stand up with him. I wouldn't like to see you fall into the hands of that set. Fortune hunters, every one of them," he said with a tsk of disgust.

"That vice is hardly limited to the French," she said, with heavy irony.

"Who is to say they're noblemen? No one decent bothers with them. You don't want to have much to do

115

with that set, Cousin. Dirty dishes, the lot of them. You'll not find them in the *Almanach de Gotha*. I expect you're planning your own ball by this time. You want to settle on a date before all the good ones are taken. Has Luten decided on his theme this year? I always look forward to his balls. I daresay it won't be a masquerade party, as he's already had that do at the Pantheon."

"Luten always keeps his theme a secret, unless a special costume is required, of course."

The conversation floundered. When Corinne offered wine, Gaviston rose and said with a raised eyebrow, "A little early in the day for me. I must be running along."

She didn't try to detain him, but she did wonder at his calling on her at all. Why not just send a footman with Harry's reply? Gaviston had been angling to discover something. Probably whether Luten had offered for her. That rumor surfaced from time to time. The putting forward of Harry as a suitor suggested it.

She soon forgot Gaviston's visit. Her thoughts turned again to whether Harry had stolen the pearls, and killed Rose and Robinson. She could no more believe it than she could believe Gaviston had done it. Baxter would clear Harry once and for all, and they could get on with discovering who was really responsible.

Chapter Fifteen

"Did Harry accept your invitation?" Luten asked Corinne. Luten, Prance and Coffen had gone to her house after their morning's work.

"Yes, Gaviston stopped by to deliver Harry's acceptance."

Gaviston was of no concern to Luten. He wasn't suspected of any crime, and as he had just become engaged to Lady Angela, he was no romantic competition.

"We must decide who is to make up the party," he said. "Harry and yourself, Prance, Coffen. The box holds six." He turned to the gentlemen. "You can both invite a lady."

"Are you not coming?" Corinne asked him, surprised.

"I'll be in the pit to keep an eye on Baxter," he replied. "He can use my opera glasses to get a good look at Harry. Baxter's itching for revenge. He might do something farouche when he sees Harry. I mean to have a Bow Street Runner on hand to make the arrest."

Corinne listened, observing how certain Luten was that Harry was guilty. He was actually enjoying this!

"That will provide society with an additional spectacle," Prance said. "Do avoid a vulgar display in Corinne's box, if possible, Luten. It hardly seems a polite place to invite a lady friend for the evening."

"There won't be any fuss," Luten said. "I suggest you all go to the corridor for a walk at the first intermission. Walk toward the staircase. I'll have the Bow Street

Officer there, waiting. I expect Harry will go quietly. He won't be eager for public humiliation."

"Cheer up," Coffen said gently to Corinne, who listened in glum silence. "There's no saying Harry is the lad we're after. We ought to have a signal, Luten, to tell us Baxter's verdict."

"Yes, a warning that Baxter has positively identified Harry, so that we shall be on the *qui vive*," Prance added. "You could wave a handkerchief. Red for yea, white for nay."

"This isn't one of your dramatic presentations," Luten said. "A simple shake of the head will do. A nod if Harry is our man, a shake if he's not."

Prance sulked. "That's hardly original."

Coffen, whose fancy soared closer to the ground, said, "Who are you going to take with you, Prance?"

"Whoever is available at such short notice. Not one of the season's more outstanding beauties, but I draw the line at an antidote. Miss Walgrave, perhaps. She's a neighbor of mine in the country. Her mama has called on me twice. The gel made her debut last season. No takers. She's well enough of face, but no conversation beyond provincial banalities. She'll do admirably for the theater. She will decorate the box without interrupting the performance."

"There's two Miss Walgraves out this year. Which one are you taking?" Coffen asked.

"There is only one Miss Walgrave, Pattle. Her sister, Miss Alice, is also making her curtsey this spring. It would be a kindness—and convenient—if you asked Miss Alice."

"What does she look like? Is she pretty?"

Prance gave the question due consideration before delivering his verdict. He did not dismiss aesthetic matters lightly. "Rather like a squirrel," he said. "Those full cheeks, you know, and small too, with darting eyes and a nervous way."

Coffen considered this. "Could be worse. I mean to say, she ain't a porker at least. Is she taller than me?"

"A regular squab. She wouldn't come past your ear."

"Good. I got a crick in my neck shouting up at that ladder you got for me the last time. I'd have a better chance of getting Miss Alice to accompany me if she don't see me first."

"You are too modest, Pattle!" Prance said, and spoiled the compliment by adding, "At ten thousand per annum, a gentleman need not be handsome. Ten thousand covers a multitude of sins."

"True," Coffen said, unoffended. "Will you do the pretty for me—ask her?"

"Oh very well. We might as well both use my carriage."

Luten frowned. "That leaves Corinne alone with Harry."

"Only to go to the theater," Prance said. "He doesn't suspect our trick. He'll behave. She shan't be coming home with him unless he's innocent, in which case she's in no danger of anything—but a little lovemaking," he added mischievously.

"I'm not afraid of Harry," Corinne said.

"I want one of you in the carriage with her at all times," Luten insisted.

Prance tsk'd in annoyance. "It will look very odd to Mrs. Walgrave if we take both daughters, and don't go in the same rig. I don't want to give her the notion I'm courting her gel."

"Then take someone else," Luten said.

After a good deal of discussion it was decided that Prance would invite Miss Walgrave and Miss Alice to the theater, both to be delivered in his carriage, while Coffen went with Harry and Corinne and met up with Miss Alice at Covent Garden. They would meet at Luten's house after they had taken the ladies home, and presumably after Lord Harry had been arrested.

Prance and Coffen left, discussing important matters of toilette for the evening. It was only on those rare occasions when Coffen was escorting a lady that he could be coerced into doing anything about his appearance, and Prance meant to make the most of this opportunity.

Luten sat beside Corinne on the sofa. He made an instinctive move to take her hand, then pulled back. "I know you're not happy with these arrangements, Corinne, but something must be done, you know," he said gruffly.

"You invented this scheme of forged pearls out of whole cloth. There's no real evidence of it. Harry isn't that bad."

Luten's attitude hardened. "The only man in London who could have made a forgery good enough to fool their owner was murdered last December," he said.

"Murdered!" She put her head in her hands and moaned. "Oh God, not another! Is there no end to it?"

When Luten spoke, his tone was softer. "With luck, tonight will be the end. You mustn't feel too badly for Harry. He's a clever deceiver, who smiles while planning how to rob and murder."

Corinne listened and finally accepted that Harry must be the guilty party, but her chest felt heavy with sorrow.

"You're right. I didn't tell you, because I wanted to protect Harry, but this wouldn't be the only time he's stolen from me. Just this week he took a Meissen box to pawn. He gave it back last night, but—actually, a few things were missing from my trinket box after I returned from that year at Appleby Court. Nothing of any value. I had my jewels locked in the safe, but a little garnet ring was missing, and a marcasite brooch. They were things from home, not grand enough for my new life. I blamed Millie Bliss—she was a new servant working for me at that time. She left while I was at Appleby. It's hard to think of Harry rifling through my private possessions. . . ."

Luten's first anger at her having protected Harry was

softened by her confession, and her sorrow. This wasn't the time to be savage with her.

"A life of crime begins with small steps—taking pennies from a mother's purse. As the fellow grows older, his needs rise apace, and he steals larger sums, or more valuable items."

"I would have said something to Harry, but I really thought it was Millie Bliss. Of course I knew it wasn't Millie who had taken the Meissen box. Harry said he had planned to pawn it and later return it."

"The little box your sister gave you?"

"Yes, I cherish it for sentimental reasons. I daresay he stole the French vase that he said was broken as well while I was at Appleby. He offered to pay."

"He's a complete hand. Confessing to that one small crime established his honesty in your eyes."

"I expect you're right." She sighed and stared off into the distance.

Luten reached for her fingers and they sat together, just holding hands in silence. After a moment, she asked, "How did he kill this other man, the one who made the forged pearls?"

Luten told her about the break in, and about Lefty Muldoon being hung for the crime.

Corinne looked up, startled. "Perhaps Lefty Muldoon was guilty! Surely they wouldn't hang him without good evidence."

How eager she was to whitewash Harry! "Evidence can be arranged. Harry might have sold one of the stolen pieces to Lefty, then sent an anonymous tip to Bow Street that Lefty had it. I wager Harry has Lefty's blood on his hands, as well as Rose Grimm's and Robinson's. I fear you must brace yourself for his arrest, Corinne."

"It will be painful for the family. Lady Angela won't like it either. I mentioned Gaviston was here this morning. He said Lady Angela didn't care for Harry's friends. Gaviston doesn't care a brass button about his own brother. He's too busy making a parade of his charity to strangers. Charity begins at home. He's never taken any interest in Harry. The whole family have always favored Gaviston, because he's the heir."

Luten's patience broke. His answer was more of a tirade than anything else. "No, because he's the more responsible of the two. Gaviston makes himself useful to society. Harry does nothing but idle away his time. Having no expectations, he should have made a career for himself—the army or the diplomatic corps—instead of robbing his friends and disgracing his family. I really cannot comprehend your championing of that scoundrel."

He fully expected Corinne to counter attack. When her head hung meekly, he was sorry for having ripped up at her.

"You're right. I must be a very bad judge of character, Luten. Harry was always my favorite of all George's relatives."

"Thank you," he said stiffly.

"Oh I didn't mean you, Luten! I forgot George was your cousin."

Her apologetic face won her a pardon. "Rogues like Harry can be charming," he said forgivingly. "That's how they gain people's trust. I must go now, Corinne. Are you going to be all right?"

"I'll be fine. You're going to Bow Street?"

"There, and to tell Baxter that his presence will be necessary at Covent Garden tonight."

"I hope nothing happens to Baxter."

"It won't. I've taken precautions."

He explained about his footman, then he left, and Corinne went up to her room and lay on the bed, beyond tears. She remembered the many occasions when she and Harry had gone about London together, laughing and happy. And all the time he was using her. They went where he wanted; they had always taken her carriage; she had paid for everything. But at least she had real friends. Luten, Prance, Coffen. Luten had been very patient with her, but she still found it hard to suspect Harry of murder.

Chapter Sixteen

Prance's valet had brushed, buffed and polished Coffen Pattle into a more acceptable mode. He came, arrayed in an unwrinkled black jacket and a cravat neither extravagantly complicated nor unstylishly simple, to take Corinne to Covent Garden. His cheeks were innocent of either those odd patches of whiskers that his own Raven usually missed, or the nicks resulting when Coffen requested—he never demanded—that his valet have another go at his face. The delicate perfume wafting from him held a hint of lilacs and lime, but by no means overpowered the nostrils.

"Coffen! How fine you look! Have you got a new valet?"

"Thankee kindly. No, I haven't turned Raven off. I'd like to. I've tried from time to time, but in the end I haven't the heart for it. Besides, he's bigger than me."

"If you're afraid to tell him, Luten would—"

"Nothing of the sort. He's an excellent man of science. He's giving me boxing lessons. I only wish he were my groom. Many a dark night I've wished Raven was with me on the box instead of Fitz. So you like the outfit? Prance's valet did me up."

"You look very tidy. It's a little early. Do sit down."

"Can't. Prance tells me it's the sitting that creases the jacket. Time enough for that at the theater. Can't stand up all through the performance, of course. I'll look like a bag of old clothes by the time we leave Covent Garden, but at least I can arrive in good curl. First impression and all that."

She assumed that Miss Alice was the cause of this new interest in sartorial matters. "Would you like some wine?"

"Best not. I might spill it on this cravat. Prance invented the arrangement. Calls it the Ultima. Ultimate what he didn't say. I hope it don't catch on. Took his man half an hour to arrange it."

"Well, we are not so very early. We can leave now, and have a visit with the deCoventrys before going to the theater."

"Don't encourage 'em. You're already asking Harry out. That's caviar to them. If you go making up to the parents, they'll announce the banns."

"I never thought of that!"

"You leave the thinking to me. We'll just stand here for ten minutes, then leave. Or I'll stand, no need for you to. Your jacket won't wrinkle since you ain't wearing one. Do you have a journal I could glance at to pass the time?"

She handed him the evening journal. He opened it to the racing news and shook his head. "Lost again. I made sure Golden Girl would win me a packet. I see Luten has won. Whoever thought a nag with a name like Lazy Boy would outrun the field? It's always the ones who don't need money that fall into it. It's the lack of blunt that did young Harry in—if he's guilty, I mean."

Corinne changed the subject. "My advertisement to the redheaded lady was in the evening journal," she mentioned.

"No word from her?"

"No. I hope we don't read of her death."

"No reason to suppose Harry knows she went to the Pantheon with Robinson. Unless Robinson told him. He did have two ticket stubs."

Corinne's eyes widened in alarm. "Dear God! I hope I

haven't put her in jeopardy. What did I write in that notice?"

She went flying about the room, and found a copy of it stuck in a magazine. She read, *"Would the redheaded lady who accompanied Mr. R. to the Pantheon charity masquerade please be in touch with the lady on Berkeley Square."*

"You didn't use her name. He'll never find her from that."

"But if he knows Robinson's redheaded friend—and if he knows I'm looking for her, he will surely kill her."

"He'll have to find her first. She's made herself pretty scarce. Now don't take a pet, Corinne. Your notice don't give anything away. And it just might bring results."

"It might get her killed!"

"Harry will be locked up before the night is over."

"And for that, I must be grateful," she said, but she didn't feel grateful, or happy, or anything but miserably apprehensive.

"Let us go," she said. She wanted to see Harry, to be sure he wasn't out scouring London for the redheaded woman.

"What's playing at the theater tonight?" Coffen asked.

"The Mourning Bride, with Mrs. Siddons."

"Good gad, it's the groom who ought to be mourning! She must be pushing sixty, and fat as a flawn."

"She doesn't play Almeria. She is Zara, the Moorish queen."

"It sounds well worth missing to me."

"I wish we weren't seeing a tragedy, with murders and suicide." Harry might commit suicide when he was caught and disgraced.

She went with a heavy heart to call on Lord Harry. Coffen accompanied her. It felt strange, going as a guest to the house that had for four years been her home. It didn't seem like home now. A coldness had settled over it. The furnishings were almost the same as before, but there were no flowers and few lamps had been lit. In the

126

saloon, Coffen sat stiff as a statue, to avoid commotion to his jacket. The whole family was there to greet Corinne. They welcomed her so politely that she realized they mistook this outing for the beginning of a courtship. Lord deCoventry opened a bottle of champagne. Lady deCoventry's sour face cracked into a smile as she said with unusual amiability what a lovely couple the youngsters made.

"So suitable as to age," she added, as a gentle reminder of Corinne's first husband. Or perhaps it was a jibe at her own husband, who favored younger lightskirts.

Through it all, Harry observed the callers with a laughing eye, and winked behind his mama's back to show Corinne he didn't consider a trip to the theater a betrothal. He seemed so relaxed and happy she couldn't believe he had murder on his conscience. Luten must be wrong about Harry.

Gaviston got her aside and said, "I see you took my little hint, Cousin. I wish Lady Angela and I could be in our box to enjoy this happy sight, but alas! Duty calls. I have a meeting with Castlereagh. He values my expertise in Austrian matters. Metternich is such a wily devil there's no trusting him."

"Duty before pleasure," she said dully.

He peered at her with concern. "I say, Cousin, is there something the matter? You don't seem your usual lively self this evening."

A guilty flush rose up her cheeks. "I'm fine, Gaviston."

"I hope it's not handing over Mama's pearls that has you so disheartened?"

"No!" she said, too loudly, too wildly. "Of course not. I—I haven't given them a thought." She read a question in his gaze, and wondered if he had heard the rumors.

Harry caught her eye and came forward. "Time to go, Corinne. Goodnight, all." He took her arm and rushed out of the room. "What nonsense has Gaviston been pouring in your ear? You looked ready to crown him with the poker. You'd best not invite me out again or we shall find ourselves tied up wing and leg."

When he noticed Coffen sliding so stiffly into the carriage, he said, "Have you hurt yourself, Pattle? What happened, get thrown from your nag?"

"No. I don't want to disturb my jacket."

"Foolish of me to ask," Harry replied, with a bewildered look at Corinne. "Who else is of the party?" he asked.

"Prance is bringing the Walgrave sisters," she told him.

"Are they well dowered?"

Coffen's first question about Miss Alice had been, "Is she pretty?" "I really don't know. They're friends of Sir Reggie," she replied.

"Miss Walgrave has ten thousand, Miss Alice has seven, I believe," Coffen told him.

"Ten thousand! By Jove, that's something like. She's bound to be an antidote."

"Don't bother rolling your eyes at Miss Alice. She is with me," Coffen said, rather crossly. Even with the assistance of Prance's valet, he knew he was no match for Lord Harry when it came to enticing the ladies.

"I shan't lay an eye on her," Lord Harry said lightly. "I'll throw my hanky at the ten thousand, thank you."

Corinne was relieved that the gentlemen discussed the racing results as they drove to the theater. She could think of nothing to say to Harry.

"Lazy Boy won?" Harry asked in disbelief. "Dash it, I had five pounds on Firefly." She wondered where he had got hold of the money. Was it the five pounds he'd borrowed from her, pretending it was to pay for his slippers?

Covent Garden, like Drury Lane Theater, had recently been razed to the ground and risen like a phoenix in a blaze of glory. The foyer was abustle with groups heading to their boxes. Prance was already ensconced with two pretty provincial ladies when the page boy led them to Corinne's box. Prance rose and presented the Walgrave sisters to the rest of the party. They were pretty girls with a whiff of the country in their gowns and accents.

By some means so subtle she could not quite figure it out, Harry ended up sitting beside Miss Walgrave, who seemed to find him extremely amusing. As this put him in the back row where Baxter would have difficulty seeing him, Corinne said, "You're supposed to be with me, Harry."

He joined her without any reluctance. He leaned over and whispered, "I'm on to a good thing in Miss Walgrave. She has not only ten thousand and a pretty face, she has no brothers! There's a good chance she'll inherit her papa's estate, eh?"

Harry had often said such things before, not entirely in jest. His hanging out for a rich bride was a large feature of his life, but tonight it left a bad feeling in his listener.

"You don't know anything about her character," she said.

"She's a regular greenhead. She laughed out loud at that stale old joke about Prinney being the Prince of Whales—then said she didn't know he liked swimming. What trouble could a Johnnie Raw like that get up to in the country?"

"It's city ways that ruin character," she agreed.

"That's the culprit. If Miss Walgrave would only marry me and carry me off to Surrey, I would become a very model of a provincial farmer." Then he laughed.

Corinne trained her opera glasses on the pit. Luten's height and elegance made him stand out from the motley crowd of fustian jackets below. How fine he looked! And he had been much gentler with her since her recent troubles, as if he truly cared for her. He was with Baxter, standing toward the front of the pit, where they could get a good view of the boxes when they turned around. Baxter looked uncomfortable in a jacket and cravat, and with his hair brushed back. He kept tugging at his cravat. Had Luten seen her? The opera glasses trembled in her fingers.

He was looking up at her box. He handed the glasses to Baxter. Baxter was turning around and staring up. His face was clamped in a mask of vengeance. He set the opera glasses to his eyes. As he focussed on Harry, Corinne felt the blood chill in her veins. She waited in a paralysis of anxiety, not moving, hardly breathing.

After a minute that seemed a lifetime, Baxter lowered the glasses, turned to Luten and shook his head in a negative. Luten spoke sharply to him. She could almost hear Luten asking if he was sure. They exchanged a few animated remarks, then Luten looked up and shook his head. Corinne's glasses brought his face close enough to read his expression of disbelief, and—yes, disappointment. He had wanted Harry to be guilty. But Harry was not the man who had called on Rose Grimm and murdered her. Baxter wouldn't make a mistake about that. Such a tide of relief swept over her that she felt giddy. Only then did she realize what this ordeal had taken out of her. Luten had so firmly convinced her Harry was guilty that she had trouble believing he was not.

When she turned and looked at him, he was glancing at the program, unaware of her scrutiny. She saw only his profile, and was struck at its youth and the sweetness of his mouth, which curved in a natural smile. She must have been mad to think he could murder anyone. His chronic lack of funds led him into mischief, but as she considered it, she was quite sure Harry hadn't taken the garnet ring or marcasite brooch. Cook had complained of Millie Bliss taking things from the larder. She was light-fingered. Those gaudy trinkets were the sort of thing to appeal to a servant girl.

She looked over her shoulder to Prance, who had just read Luten's signal. He nodded and whispered in Coffen's ear. Coffen's head turned to Corinne. He saw unshed tears glistening in her eyes, and a great smile of relief on her face.

The audience later agreed that the Tragic Muse had done herself proud in the role of Zara. They all thought it a remarkable achievement for a lady her age. Miss Walgrave even wept, but through it all, a smile sat on Lady deCoventry's lips. She was particularly attentive to Lord Harold. She insisted on champagne at both intermissions. It was not until nearly the end of the play that she began to consider other aspects of Harry's innocence. If he had not stolen the pearls and murdered all those people—then who had?

Coffen, who was making some headway with Miss Alice despite the rumpled state of his jacket after sitting for hours, suggested dinner at the Pulteney after the play. The Misses Walgrave regretfully declined. Their mama expected them home. Harry had wandered off to chat to some friends.

He came to Corinne as they waited for her carriage and said, "You don't mind if I go on with my chums? Dinsmore has hired a parlor at the Rose Tavern. He could get me into the FHC if I play my cards right. I wouldn't suggest it if we were alone, but since Pattle is with us—"

"Of course, Harry. Go along with your friends."

"Thank you for a lovely evening." He said a few words to Miss Walgrave, waved and ran off.

"Well, there we are, then," Coffen said, after Prance had led the Walgrave girls away. "Young Harry ain't our man. Never thought he was m'self. Do you want to go somewhere to wet your whistle, or shall we go home? I daresay Luten is there, wearing a hole in the carpet with his pacing. I notice he left at the end of the first act."

"Let us go home," she said.

Chapter Seventeen

The mêlée of traffic after the play slowed their departure, but eventually their carriage arrived and they left. To escape the rush of carriages wending their way along Piccadilly to the west end, Coffen told his groom to turn right at Glasshouse Street. The driver made the wrong turn and ended up on Sherwood Street. In his efforts to find his way back, he drove through a maze of unfamiliar streets. Although they had left the crowd behind, they were still in a civilized part of town and felt no concern. It was at the corner of Warwick and Beak Streets that Coffen pulled the drawstring.

"We've passed that corner twice. Fitz has lost his way again," he said. "I'll have a word with him." It was a familiar feature of Coffen's life that none of his servants could perform his duty satisfactorily—and Coffen was by no means a hard master.

He stuck his head out the window and called, "Go back down to Glasshouse and turn left—no, right. Dash it, go down to Piccadilly. I know my way home from—here, what do you want?"

The last words were uttered in a sharp tone. Corinne looked to the window to see what had caused it, and found herself staring at the muzzle of a pistol. She froze in terror as the man opened the door and ordered them out. He was a large, hulking man in a fustian jacket.

"Just as you like," a chastened Coffen said, and climbed down, already reaching for his purse. "No need to get snarly. Here is my purse. There's ten pounds in it."

A gloved hand reached out and seized the purse. Corinne sat with her heart pounding, waiting for her turn. The man opened Coffen's purse before making her get out. She peered through the shadows but saw only a hat pulled low over a black mask. Another masked man was at his elbow. The masks were the most frightening part of it. They called to mind the other masked man, who had stolen her pearls.

"La parure," the second man said in a low tone to his accomplice, pointing to Corinne's necklace. Diamonds and sapphires glittered in the dim moonlight. The men were French!

"Get out, Madame," the first man said, pronouncing the last word with a French accent. Madame, not Madam.

She was just bracing herself to rise when the shot rang out. Coffen's groom might not be an efficient driver, but he at least knew enough to keep a pistol under the driver's box, and he used it to good effect. The hat was lifted off the head of the man standing behind.

"Sacre bleu! Allons vite!" he exclaimed, and they both took off on foot. In her first spate of relief, Corinne didn't find it strange that two armed men were so easily discouraged.

She scrambled out of the carriage. Coffen and the coachman gave chase, but Coffen was no athlete, and by the time the groom got down from his perch, the men were gone. They had vanished between two houses, or around a corner. In the excitement and the darkness of night, no one was even sure which direction they had gone, so the pursuers returned to the carriage.

"Well done, Fitz," Coffen said to his coachman. "I'd give you a pourboire, but the scoundrel got away with my blunt."

"Tomorrow will do just fine," Fitz said, grinning.

"Thank you, Fitz," Corinne gasped. "You saved our lives."

"No such a thing," Coffen objected. "Saved your necklace. Thing to do, get out of here. Back up on your perch,

Fitz. Keep that pistol handy. And spring 'em." As he assisted Corinne into the carriage, he said, "Don't be giving Fitz ideas he's a hero. He's hard enough to handle as it is. If he had driven where I told him to, this wouldn't have happened."

Fitz cracked his whip and the carriage lurched off.

"Highwaymen are unusual in town, aren't they?" Corinne asked, frowning. "Especially this part of town."

"They weren't highwaymen. The scamps ride horses. I wouldn't mind being held up by a proper highwayman. They were nothing but footpads. A bit embarrassing."

"Why were they so easily discouraged? There were two of them, with guns. They saw my diamond necklace. They could have overpowered us."

"We won't tell anyone what happened. Feel ashamed of myself, to tell the truth. I handed over my blunt without so much as a cross word."

"Don't be foolish, Coffen. You did the right thing. They might have killed us if you had argued with them."

"That's kind of you, but I don't want Prance throwing this up in my face, pouring salt in the wound. We're just lucky Fitz kept his wits about him. If Raven had been on the box, he wouldn't have got lost. He can read a map, even when it's printed upside down, as they always are."

"Why don't Raven and Fitz switch jobs?"

"Raven's afraid of horses. One bit him when he was a tad. Won't go near 'em. Pity."

"We must tell Luten what happened, Coffen," Corinne said.

"None of his dashed business. It has nothing to do with anything. With the pearls, I mean, or the murders."

"Perhaps it has. Those men were French, like Rose's beau."

"They spoke English. At least one of 'em did."

"He spoke with an accent. And the one behind said to get my *parure*. That's French for necklace."

"Are you sure? I thought he said partner."

"I'm positive."

They reached Berkeley Square without further incident. The lights in Luten's saloon suggested that he was awaiting them there. When they entered, they found Prance had joined him. The Walgrave sisters had been delivered home, well satisfied with their evening, especially Miss Walgrave, who was looking forward to a call from Lord Harold the next day.

Luten took one look at Corinne and demanded, "What happened?" Fear lent an angry edge to his words.

"We got lost," Coffen said, with a warning glance at Corinne, and went into a longish story of how it had happened.

Prance looked from one to the other with a mischievous smile on his lips. "And now let us have the truth," he said.

Coffen lowered a darkling brow at him. "Are you calling me a liar?"

"Don't be vulgar, Pattle. I merely say you are not telling the truth."

"Oh. How did you know?"

"Getting lost doesn't cause a pallor. Corinne looks as if she's seen a ghost. She was in high feather when we parted, due to Lord Harry's presumed innocence."

"How would you expect her to look when we was set upon by—by highwaymen?" Coffen said.

Luten jumped from his chair. "Highwaymen!" He turned to Corinne. His hands reached out and grasped her upper arms. "Are you all right?"

"Yes, they didn't get my jewelry," she said. But she knew his concern wasn't for her jewelry, and she felt a pleasant warmth rush in to ease the chill of fear.

"Highwaymen, in London?" Prance asked in a voice of patent disbelief. "Come, come, surely you mean a ragamuffin cutpurse."

"He was no ragamuffin," Coffen shot back. "And there were two of them! I hear you shaking your head, Prance. I'd like to know what *you'd* do if you had a pistol pointed at your nose."

135

"I would give the person my purse, and anything else he wanted. I expect you fell into brawling with him?"

"Nothing of the sort. I gave him my purse. The only sane thing to do. He might have killed m—Corinne."

Prance bowed. "A thousand pardons, my dear Pattle. It is the state of your jacket that led me astray. How did you manage to undo my valet's work so thoroughly?"

"I sat down. I told you what would happen."

"Quiet, you two," Luten said, and handed Corinne a glass of wine. "Now, let's hear the story properly. You'd best tell it, Corinne." He led her to a seat and sat beside her, hovering as if she might fly away. "You may omit the part about the shortcut via Glasshouse Street."

She told the story, lavishing what Coffen felt was undue praise on Fitz, and making too much of the fact that the men didn't use their pistols, but took off at Fitz's first shot.

"A couple of tyros," Prance suggested. "A cutpurse has to learn his trade, like anyone else."

"You think they were Frenchmen?" Luten asked Corinne.

"I'm sure of it."

"The lad's name was English," Coffen said.

Luten and Prance stared at him in astonishment. "Did he introduce himself?" Prance asked satirically. "Leave his card, perhaps? The coves are becoming quite civilized."

"No, I heard one of 'em say to the other, Allan Veet. Allan is an English name. I know any number of Allans."

"Allons, vite?" Luten enquired, turning to Corinne.

"Exactly."

"You heard it too, then?" Coffen asked her.

"You really are remarkably ignorant, Pattle," Prance said. "It is French for 'let us shab off, quickly.' So we may take it, then, that the cutpurses were French."

"Highwaymen," Coffen insisted.

Prance waved an elegant hand. "Let us say *voleurs*. The question is, are they connected with Rose Grimm's *Monsieur?*"

136

"Of course they are," Luten said impatiently. "Any fool can see that." He turned to Corinne. Worried for her safety, he spoke roughly. "I knew you shouldn't have put that notice in the journal. The man fears you'll learn something. This attack was intended for more than a robbery; he meant to kill you, as he killed Gregory, under the guise of robbery."

Prance listened, and said, "Does it not leap to the eye that the Conte de Creuse could be involved?"

"It didn't look like him, or any of his friends," Coffen said. "These were ugly, hulking fellows."

"I thought they were masked," Prance said.

"They were rough, not gentlemen," Corinne explained. "I'm sure it wasn't de Creuse."

"Huge brutes, all of them," Coffen added.

"Surely you mean both of them. All suggests an army," Prance taunted. "Since learning of Lord Harry's innocence, we've lost our prime suspect. Fortunate the Frenchies turned up to replace him. But who are they?"

That was the question that bedeviled the Berkeley Brigade as they sat in Luten's saloon, nursing their claret.

"Baxter says Harry is not the man who called on Rose," Luten said. "The man was approximately the same size and coloring, but older than Harry. My fear was that, in his wrath, Baxter would put his finger on the first suspect offered. I was prepared for that. You could have blown me over with a feather when he said positively that Harry was not our man."

They sat a moment in silence, brooding over this development. All except Corinne, who wore a satisfied look that annoyed Luten to no small degree.

"Harry might have known the Frenchie who was seeing Rose and had him get the costume," Luten suggested, and was greeted with three derisive looks. "No, no. This is not sheer imbecility speaking. If tonight's attack was planned, then who but Harry could have planned it? He knew you were going to the theater, Corinne. He could have arranged to have thugs follow you. Come to that, why was he not in the carriage with you? How did he get home?"

"He went with some friends to the Rose Tavern," she said.

"So that was his story!"

"I saw him leave with his friends."

"You don't know how long he stayed with them."

"If he wasn't with them, then he was on foot. He went to the theater with Coffen and me."

"I'm not suggesting he personally attacked your rig. He obviously hired ruffians, as he hired Robinson to steal the pearls."

"Did he know you were wearing the pearls to the masquerade, Corinne?" Prance asked.

Before she could answer, Coffen said, "He did. I was in the saloon with you when you decided, Corrie. You said, 'And I'll have a final wear of the pearls to lend a touch of class to all this pinchbeck jewelry.' Something of the sort."

"Yes, he knew," Corinne admitted, "but he didn't have time tonight—"

Luten said, "Before you say the highwaymen didn't have time to follow you from the theater, let me remind you that the traffic moves by inches when the play lets out. Men on foot could easily have overtaken you."

"I see a flaw in your reasoning, Luten, if you will pardon my saying so," Prance said. He rose and began to pace daintily to and fro before the grate as he spoke.

"Our malefactor does not do things by halves. He is nothing if not thorough. *Vide* his elimination of all witnesses. Would such a man hire amateurs to hold up Corinne? If they were after her *parure*, or if their intention, God forbid, was to kill her, one has the sense that they would have succeeded." He turned to Corinne. "I'm sorry if I frightened you, my pet, but we must be brutally honest. It's possible someone is trying to kill you, but it is my contention that he wouldn't have been distracted from the job by one shot that missed its mark."

Coffen bristled up like a bear. "There's no reason to frighten the wits out of the poor girl. No one is trying to kill Corinne. He could have shot her easily. And me too. He had the dashed pistol stuck right in my nose."

Prance threw up his hands. "I hope you may be right," he said, and lifted his coattails to sit down.

"As I was saying about young Harry," Luten began.

Corinne just shook her head. "Leave it go, Luten. Harry is innocent. He didn't steal the pearls, and he didn't kill Rose."

"Then why was Gregory murdered?" Luten countered. "Only Harry had easy access to the pearls during that year you were away. He had Gregory make forgeries, and murdered him to conceal the fact."

"Oh really! Harry's become an obsession with you. We don't even know the pearls were forgeries. I'm sure the ones I wore to the masquerade were my own genuine pearls."

"Actually Lord deCoventry's," Coffen said.

She gave him a testy look. "You know what I mean. Lefty Muldoon tried to rob the shop, Gregory caught him in the act and Muldoon shot him."

"I fear she's right," Prance said. "What establishment is more likely to be robbed than a jewelry shop? Gregory's death has nothing to do with the pearls, nor has tonight's attack by French footpads, necessarily. There is such a thing as coincidence. We are struggling through a shoal of red herrings. 'When sorrows come, they come not single spies, but in battalions.' One can always count on dear Shakespeare to have said the truth, and in a manner beyond improvement."

" 'To be or not to be,' " Coffen murmured, his sole familiarity with Shakespeare.

"We're no closer to finding the thief than we were at the beginning," Corinne said, "and I have to return the pearls on Friday."

"Either that or marry Lord Harry," Coffen added. Everyone looked at him in confusion. "As a last resort, I mean," he said. "Pretty clear that's what the family wants. Pleased as punch at your inviting Harry out, Corinne. Broke open the champagne and all. They'd forget the pearls fast enough if you offered for Harry. Maybe they stole them to force your hand."

"Has he done it again, had an idea?" Prance asked, looking around.

"Marry Harold!" Luten exclaimed. "Leap from the frying pan into the fire, you mean!" He mistrusted Corinne's smile.

"No, even the deCoventrys are not that foolish. Corinne could marry anyone," Prance said. "So, what is to be done?"

"Don't know about you lot," Coffen said, rising, "but I plan to hang around de Creuse's place tomorrow and see if I can spot the highwaymen. They weren't him, but they might call on him."

"You do that," Prance said. "Be sure you take Fitz along to rescue you, should another street urchin demand your purse."

"I don't have a purse. The highwaymen have already got it." On that speech, Coffen left, feeling he had given Prance a pretty good setdown.

"Nothing more to be done tonight," Prance said, rising and stretching his arms. "I shall see you home, my pet." He offered Corinne his hand.

"I'll take Corinne home," Luten said.

They all left together, Prance to make the short dart home, and Luten to lead Lady deCoventry across the road.

"It's been quite a night, has it not?" he asked, when they reached her doorway.

"It's been quite a week."

"You're relieved that Harry is innocent, I expect?"

"Indeed I am. I couldn't believe—but I did believe it, in the end. That's what this is doing to us, making us distrust old friends."

"Is he such a good friend, when he robbed you on more than one occasion?"

"I don't think he did—except for the little Meissen box, and he returned it."

"I hope you aren't thinking of following Coffen's advice and marrying him?" he asked, trying to sound facetious.

Corinne detected the glint of concern behind the joke, and decided to let him know her feelings about Harry. "It would seem incestuous. Harry's like a brother to me."

Luten smiled, satisfied. "And besides, it's forbidden by the Table of Kindred and Affinity in the *Book of Common Prayer*. I daresay deCoventry could get around it, but nephew by marriage is the last item in the Table of Kindred."

"How do you come to know that obscure fact?"

"I looked it up."

"Why?" she asked, with a quizzing look.

"A family matter," he said in a dismissing way. When she went on smiling, he added, "Cousin Aurelia and Cousin Hammond—I don't believe you've met them?"

She didn't believe they existed. "Odd George never mentioned them, but if they are in the same relation as Harry and myself, Gaviston tells me it can be arranged, since there is no actual blood kinship in such a tenuous connection."

"Gaviston said so, did he?"

"Yes, perhaps he was checking on behalf of Aurelia and Hammond as well." Her smile was as good as an invitation.

Luten drew her slowly into his arms, expecting at every second that she'd pull back. In all their long acquaintance, it was the first time he had embraced her. When he proposed at Appleby Court, he had only loved her from afar. And when she had rejected him, laughed at him, his pride had prevented any further romantic overtures. A mask of cynicism had covered his hurt. He hardly knew what to expect now, but at least he knew she wouldn't laugh at him, when she needed his help.

He wasn't prepared for the warmth of her response.

141

She went willingly, almost eagerly into his arms, as if she'd been waiting a long time for this. He gazed at her questioningly, and was answered by a silent, provocative shimmer from her dark eyes. Her lips trembled open in an encouraging smile. Without further ado, Luten lowered his head. His lips brushed hers lightly, tentatively, waiting to see how she would react.

At the first touching of their lips, a spark leapt between them and burst into flame. She looped her arms around his neck. His arms tightened instinctively, crushing her against his chest as if he'd never let her go. As his lips firmed in passion, she returned every sweet pressure of his desire. It had happened so quickly, so unexpectedly that neither of them quite understood, or believed it. For a moment the universe shrank to the two square feet of pavement where they stood, clinging desperately to each other. Then as suddenly as the embrace had begun, she drew back and gazed at him with wild eyes.

Smiling, she said, "Well, that was unexpected. I've felt so helpless lately. I just needed someone to hang on to."

"Hang on to me," he said in a husky voice, and kissed her again with a ruthless, punishing passion.

Corinne felt pierced through with a dizzying joy. George's tame embraces were the only man's love she had ever known. She had no idea it could be like this. Thought was obliterated, transformed to an exultant flight of rapture as Luten's strong arms held her tight and safe against him. Dear Luten! How had she thought he disliked her? She couldn't be mistaken about this feeling. He felt it too, this pleasure so intense it was almost a pain.

She drew back again and gazed at him with a drugged smile. "I never knew it—could be so—"

"I always knew it could be, with you," he said. He was within a heartbeat of proposing. But it would be ungentlemanly to offer marriage when she felt beholden to him. Better to leave it until the mystery was solved. He didn't want her memories of their engagement to be tainted with such unpleasant associations.

He raised her hand to his lips and pressed a kiss on her fingers. He gazed at her pale face, bathed in moonlight, and made a foolish promise. "We'll find out who did all these awful things, dearest. That's a promise. Now I'll let you go to bed. Sweet dreams."

He placed a light kiss on her cheek and opened the door. When she was safely inside with the door locked, Luten returned to his own house, marveling at how easily and naturally they had finally acknowledged their love. It was not until he was inside that he began to wonder how he could fulfill his rash promise.

Chapter Eighteen

When Corinne opened her eyes the next morning and saw the dull glow behind her green curtains, she thought it must be early. A glance at her clock showed her it was half past eight. It was a dull day, then. No sunshine. She knew Mrs. Ballard would soon be at her door with the morning cocoa. During the few moments while she awaited her arrival, Corinne mentally added up how much time she had to find the pearls. Two more days— and they were no closer to finding them than they had been the night they were stolen.

Mrs. Ballard tapped lightly at the door and came in, smiling. "A nasty day out there," she said, setting down the tray. "I had planned to sit in the garden and read, but I believe I shall get caught up on my correspondence instead. There's a little parcel there on your tray. Black said to give it to you. I'm afraid he must have spilt something on it. The paper is wet."

"Thank you, Mrs. Ballard," Corinne said distractedly. Mrs. Ballard drew the curtains, shook her head at the rain and glided out.

Corinne picked up the little parcel, no bigger than a sugarplum. It was wrapped in common newspaper, wet, as Mrs. Ballard had said. Corinne's heart rose up to her throat. She could think of only one thing that would come in such a small parcel—a ring. Luten had sent over the family engagement ring! But what an odd way to do it, wrapped in common newsprint! Her fingers trembled as she tore at the paper. When she saw what it contained, a spontaneous gasp of astonishment issued from her lips.

It was a pearl. Just one perfect pearl, and if her memory was right, it was from her stolen necklace. The size was certainly right. She examined it closely, to make sure it wasn't a fake pearl. It looked genuine. Her breath was coming in short gasps as she ferreted through the wrapping to see if there was a note. The sodden paper fell apart as she handled it. The note was there, just a few lines scribbled on rough paper. *If you are wanting the rest of them, meet me at the Green Man just this side of Maidstone at three this afternoon.*

Corinne leapt out of bed and ran to her door. "Mrs. Ballard!" she called. "Please ask Luten to come over at once!"

Mrs. Ballard's head peeped out of her doorway. "What is it, milady? Not bad news, I hope?"

"No, good news."

Mrs. Ballard trotted downstairs to give the message. Corinne threw on her traveling suit of pomona green, ran a brush through her hair, gathered up the pearl, the note and the wrapping and went downstairs to await Luten. She got a magnifying glass from the study and examined the pearl. Peering into the hole made for the golden wire, she was certain the pearl was genuine. If it were a fish-paste pearl, she would be able to see where the coating stopped and the glass bead began.

When she was sure it was genuine, she went for a word with Black. "That little package, Black, who delivered it? Did it come with the morning post?"

"It didn't, milady. It was an odd thing. When I opened the door to have a look out at the weather, there it sat on the doorstep, wedged into the corner. It was just the way it was when I gave it to you, wrapped up in newsprint. Soaking wet it was, as if it had been there some time. This little card was stuck in beside it." He handed her the card. *For Lady deCoventry* was printed in ink that was faded from the rain.

145

She took the card. "You didn't see who—"

He shook his head. "It might have been there since I locked the door last night, milady. There's no knowing."

"I see. Thank you. Send Luten to me as—"

Even while she spoke, Luten came in, without knocking. He took one look at Corinne and said, "Has something happened?"

"Bring coffee to the study, Black," Corinne said, and led Luten to her study. The room was no oak-paneled affair with heavy furnishings, but a lady's dainty study. The wainscotting had been painted a creamy white, with a green patterned paper above. The desk was a delicate mahogany piece with a set of three matching chairs. The one behind the desk was padded and had arms.

Corinne handed the package, note and all, to Luten. "Black found this on the doorstep this morning," she said. "It's genuine. I looked at it with the magnifying glass. I'm sure it's from my necklace. The size, the lustre—everything matches."

Luten glanced at the pearl and card but read the note first, frowning as he read it a second time. "Demmed odd," he said. "There's no mention of what price the fellow wants. Surely he doesn't plan to hand the necklace over gratis."

Then he took the pearl and magnifying glass and studied the bored hole, as Corinne had done. "It seems genuine," he said. "I could run it down to Pennyworth, but then I don't like to stir up unnecessary talk."

"It's genuine," she said. "Who could have sent it?"

"We won't know that until we meet him at the Green Man."

"You'll come with me?"

"You don't think I'd let you go alone! The note doesn't say anything about your going alone. That's odd too."

"It almost seems as if this is from a friend, who just wants to return the pearls," she said, looking for Luten's reaction.

"That's hard to believe. Why did he steal them, if he only plans to give them back?"

"We think Robinson stole them. He's dead." The coffee arrived. Corinne poured two cups and handed one to Luten. "I was thinking of the redhead. She might have got the pearls from Robinson before he was killed."

"If she stole them from him, she's not planning to give them back without making something on the deal."

"We'll just have to wait and see what she asks. In any case, this does away once and for all with the notion that someone had fake pearls made. If this is from the stolen necklace, then the necklace is genuine."

They heard footsteps in the hallway.

"Prance has been watching at the window again and come running to see what's afoot," Luten said.

The door opened to reveal not only Prance but also Coffen, both with their eyes wide open and looking exceedingly curious. Prance was still carrying a violet umbrella against the rain. He leaned it against the desk. Coffen's hair and shoulders were sprinkled with raindrops.

"What ho?" Prance exclaimed, spotting the pearl in Luten's fingers. "A new development?"

Luten handed him the pearl and magnifying glass. "What's your opinion of this, Reg?" Luten asked. Prance put the pearl between his teeth and tested it. He then applied the glass to the hole and declared, "Genuine. Not a doubt. It's from the necklace, of course. Where did you get it?"

Coffen had helped himself to the note. He handed it to Prance. "Sounds suspicious to me," he said. "Why does he want to meet her so far away? Maidstone's forty miles from here. Could be an ambush. We can't let Corinne go alone."

"The writer doesn't ask her to go alone," Luten pointed out.

Prance studied the note. "Nor does he mention what sum he's demanding for the pearls. Stranger and stranger. The wording of the note is a little odd, too. 'If you are wanting the rest of them.' Why not 'If you want the rest of them'?"

"Why 'if' at all?" Coffen said. "He knows she wants them right enough."

"No, no. You miss my point," Prance said. "This use of the present progressive tense is not idiomatic English. In English we can say, *par example*, I go, I do go and I am going. The French say only *je vais*. They have only the one present tense. They don't know quite how to handle our plethora of choices. What I am suggesting, I think, is that this was written by a Frenchman."

"That would explain this, then," Coffen said, and laid a piece of the outer wrapping on the desk. "It's French, ain't it?"

Prance carefully picked up the scrap of paper and read from its small surface. "*Quant à—aucun doute* . . . Yes, it's a fragment from a French journal. Well, how very *intéressant*. He's making no effort at all to hide his identity. Of course if he plans to meet with Corinne, he knows his accent will betray him. Who will go with her? All of us, since no embargo has been put on her?" he asked, looking around.

"A crowd might put her off," Corinne said uncertainly.

"Her?" Prance asked at once, and was told Corinne's idea.

"A woman might very well write such an unclear note as this. I expect it is Luten you will want to accompany you, Corinne, since it was him you called," he said with a pout.

"Why don't you and Coffen see what you can learn about the more raffish French element here in London?" Luten suggested.

"I wouldn't even know where to ask about the raffish element," Prance declared.

"I already planned to keep an eye on de Creuse," Coffen mentioned. "What time are you two leaving?"

"Soon," Luten replied. "I'd like to be there a good hour before the Frenchman—or woman," he added with

148

a smile to Corinne, "arrives. We don't want to be caught off guard. And with this rain, it might be a slow trip."

"Will you take money with you, to buy the pearls?" Prance asked.

"I wouldn't if I was you. Might be a plot to rob you, since they didn't get Corinne's diamonds last night," Coffen said.

"Good thinking," Luten said. "I can always make arrangements at a bank in Maidstone, if threats don't work, and if the pearls are for sale at a reasonable price." He turned to Corinne. "When would you like to leave?"

"It's nine o'clock. Say, three hours to get there. You want to be an hour early—"

"We'll want to leave a little leeway, bearing in mind the weather," Luten mentioned. "With a stop for lunch— I'd say we should leave as soon as you're ready."

"I don't envy you your trip," Prance said, and went home in a miff, clutching his violet umbrella.

Coffen drank Corinne's coffee and toddled off a moment later.

"I'll go home and order my carriage," Luten said.

"I'll get my pelisse and meet you at the carriage," Corinne said, and went to prepare for the trip.

She felt the redheaded woman had read her notice in the journal. Perhaps she had removed to Maidstone for safety's sake. This suggested that the redhead was French. Well, why not? None of them had heard her speak. She might not demand any money at all, but Corinne meant to give her a generous reward.

149

Chapter Nineteen

The rain did not delay their trip, but it took a good deal of the pleasure out of it. Luten drove his hunting carriage. They took the Old Kent Road through the Garden of England, famous for its natural beauty. The orchards were in bloom, but their clouds of blossom were blurred by the curtain of water. The outline of the oast houses with their pointed ventilating cowls could be seen but the poles holding the hops faded into the surrounding green mist.

The coachman set a slowish pace over the rain-slicked road. Their errand was too important, and the weather too unpleasant, to lend any air of romance to the trip. In the carriage, Luten and Corinne discussed the note and the pearl until they could think of no more to say. It was after one o'clock when they arrived at the Green Man.

It was a small, ancient building dating from the days of Henry VIII. Its bottom half was a hotch-potch of flint and stone, the top half brick and timber, with leaded windows. Luten identified himself and his companion as soon as they entered, and asked if anyone had been asking for Lady deCoventry.

"No, milord," the proprietor said. "It's been a quiet morning. The weather—"

"We'd like a private parlor. And if someone is asking for Lady deCoventry, I would appreciate it if you would notify us before telling them we're here." A golden coin passed from Luten's hand to the proprietor's as they shook hands.

"You want me to tell him you're here?" the man asked in confusion. He had assumed this was an illicit tryst.

"Oh certainly!" Corinne said. "It may be a woman. Tell her—tell her we are expected soon, and notify us at once."

"In the meanwhile, we'll have some lunch," Luten added.

Corinne was ravenously hungry after missing her breakfast. An hour was spent over a leisurely lunch of raised pigeon pie, ham and a few side dishes. A bottle of claret helped ease the tension. They dawdled over coffee, glancing often at their watches. By two-thirty the rain had stopped and a weak ray of sunshine struggled through the small leaded windows.

Luten took up a position there, where he could watch the main road. A few carriages came into the inn yard, raising hopes that the writer of the letter had arrived, but in each case, it proved to be only a traveler or a local stopping for an ale.

"It won't be long now," Luten said at three o'clock.

"I'm sorry we came so early," Corinne said. "I'm growing roots."

Luten went out to speak to the proprietor. When he returned, he said, "There was no message. I thought perhaps something was delaying our—friend."

"She may have enquired at the stable and left when she learned I came with you. I should have come alone."

"The note didn't say so. I'll have a word with my groom."

Luten was glad to escape the small parlor for a few minutes in the sun. His groom assured him that no one had enquired as to the owner of the hunting carriage. Nothing resembling a French accent had been heard.

Luten returned to tell Corinne the no news. He borrowed a pack of cards and ordered more wine, and they played cards to pass the time. At four o'clock he said, "It begins to look as if no one is coming."

"Let us stay a little longer, just in case."

151

Luten agreed, but he was beginning to think this was all a wild goose chase. By four-thirty, their nerves were as tight as fiddle strings.

"No one is coming," Luten said.

"So it seems. Let us go. This has been a dreadful waste of time."

Corinne spent the trip home with her eyes glued to the window, hoping to see the redheaded woman dashing, late, to the Green Man. Luten was in a foul mood by then. He felt a pronounced urge to rip up at someone, but when he saw the dispirited slump of his companion's shoulders, he controlled his anger and even tried to comfort her.

At twilight, the carriage drove into Berkeley Square. Within minutes, Coffen and Prance came darting into Corinne's saloon to demand what had transpired.

"She didn't come," Corinne said, and dropped onto the striped sofa with a weary sigh.

"It was a ruse," Luten said grimly.

"Perhaps a trick to get you out of town for the day," Prance suggested. He had spent the past hour with his valet, and was primped and perfumed for the evening. His elegance was at odds with the rumpled state of the others.

"Less than two more days now before I have to turn over the pearls," Corinne said.

"Best pour her a glass of wine," Coffen said in an aside to Prance. "Her bottom lip's wobbling. She'll be in tears soon."

Prance poured wine for them all.

"Any news here?" Corinne asked, accepting the wine.

"Nothing regarding the pearls," Prance said. "Just the usual social nothings." He turned to Coffen. "You were to watch de Creuse and company. Any action there?"

"Lord Harry dropped in on them."

Luten leapt from his chair. "Harry? What—"

"Nothing in it though," Coffen said. "I waited until he came out and had a word with him. He gave a pretty

152

good account of himself. DeCoventry had sent him to warn de Creuse away from Corinne. As head of the family, you know. Just the sort of thing he would do."

"It made a good excuse, in any case," Luten said.

"A reason, not an excuse," Prance objected. "I thought one of us should hint de Creuse away if he called on Corinne."

"Harry has agreed to peddle their medals and what not for them," Pattle said. "That don't look as if they're sitting on a string of pearls worth a fortune. Harry's going to take the stuff to the British Museum. Thinks they might be interested in it. He's taking a twenty-five percent commission. He didn't try to dodge at all when he saw me. I think Harry is all right."

"Of course he's all right," Corinne said. "Baxter proved that last night."

"He proved Harry did not personally murder Rose," Luten said. "He may have hired a Frenchie to do it for him."

"Did all that business not have to do with Harry's having stolen the pearls and replaced them with a set of fakes?" Prance asked. "We now have some evidence the pearls that were stolen are genuine. There's no more reason to suspect Harry than anyone else. Less. We know he didn't murder Rose."

"He might have stolen them to sell for cash," Luten insisted.

Corinne's patience broke at his persisting that Harry was involved. "Harry is my friend," she said. "If he only meant to steal some jewelry, I am the last one he would prey on," she said.

"It seems to me you would be the first," Luten countered.

She gave him a warning look. If he revealed Harry's little theft of the Meissen box, she would never speak to him again.

Prance sensed some unspoken message between them. "Why do you say that?" he asked.

"Because any sane lady would report him," Luten said. "He counts on Corinne's goodwill not to prosecute."

"If Harry needed money desperately, he knew I would be glad to lend it to him," she said.

"You're hardly in a position to lend him ten thousand pounds."

"He wouldn't need ten thousand pounds. Good gracious, the most he ever borrowed is ten pounds."

"The moneylenders would never have lent Harry such a sum," Coffen said. "Harry's out of it. Let's put our minds to finding who did do it."

"And why you were led on this merry chase today," Prance added. "It gave the thief and murderer one more day to cover his trail—or to get away."

"Slip out of the country with the necklace," Coffen said.

"Let us put this wasted afternoon behind us and decide what to do this evening," Prance suggested. "Come to me for dinner. I took the liberty, Corinne, of asking André to prepare your favorite *côtelettes de mouton à l'Irandlaise*, and a *pôtage de poissons à la Russe*."

"Fish soup, in other words," Coffen muttered.

"That's very kind of you, Reg," she said. "I must go and change, and have a word with Mrs. Ballard."

"I also took the liberty of telling her you would dine with me," Prance said. "She has elected to remain here. A touch of the megrims, she said, though I suspect it is only an aversion to André's cuisine. I trust you are all coming?" he said, looking at the others. Luten nodded his acceptance.

"I'll wait here and take Corinne across," Prance said, since he had already changed for the evening.

It was decided over dinner that the Brigade would split up that evening to cover more territory. Luten didn't announce his destination, but he planned to follow Harry and see where he went. Once they were away from Corinne, he told Coffen he was to follow de Creuse and company. Prance declared that Corinne was too overwrought to do more than sit in a quiet theater box. He would accompany her to the Royal Coburg, on the Surrey side of the Thames, where he was curious to see what his friend Almont was doing with a revival of Sheridan's *The Rivals*.

"A sparkling comedy will cheer you up," he said.

It cheered Prance no end to see what a botch Almont made of it. Whoever thought it would be possible to produce a dull version of Sheridan? But Almont had succeeded beyond his wildest hopes.

Luten was less satisfied with his night. Harry did nothing more suspicious than pay a visit to Miss Walgrave, from whence he went to a rout alone, and left an hour later with a couple of bucks to spend the remainder of the evening at the Rose Tavern.

Luten met Coffen at the latter's house at one, where he learned de Creuse and the other *contes* had neither gone out nor had any callers.

"I peeked in the windows. What they was doing was pressing their jackets—in their saloon, and washing out their small cloths in the kitchen sink. Poor blighters. I believe I shall buy a couple of them medals from Harry after all. Mean to say, washing their own linen."

The downstairs of Corinne's house was in darkness when Luten left Coffen. A light burned in her bedchamber, suggesting that Corinne had returned from the theater and retired. Black always stayed up to wait for her. Like all the other men in London, he was in love with her. All except the scoundrel who had stolen her pearls. Luten still harbored the secret conviction that Lord Harry was at the bottom of it. His evening had been innocent, but he had had all day to get up to mischief. Was that why Corinne had been sent off on that wild goose chase to the Green Man? But if he had stolen the genuine pearls, where did he hope to sell them? He must know every fence and jewelry shop in London was on the lookout for them. It had to be France. That was why he was working his way into the confidence of the French *contes*.

Luten's night had been extremely uncomfortable and boring, lurking about outside of houses and clubs. He'd pass the job along to a couple of his servants tomorrow.

Corinne's night had also been tedious. She wasn't in a mood for the theater, and Prance had been particularly annoying, complaining at every line of the play. When she returned home, Black had handed her a note.

"Who is it from?" she asked.

"She didn't leave her name, milady. A redheaded woman called. I wouldn't call her a lady. She seemed most eager to see you."

Corinne reached for the note with trembling fingers.

Chapter Twenty

The note was brief. Though no copperplate model of a lady's penmanship, it was not crudely written either.

I read your advert in the journal. Meet me in Hyde Park tomorrow at noon if you want to know who had Robinson steal your pearls. Come alone. Dismount from your carriage and walk about the park. I know you. I will find you.

There was no signature.

"Is everything all right, milady?" Black enquired. Having already read the note, he expected a shout of joy, but saw only a frown. "Shall I send for Lord Luten?"

"No! Black, the woman who delivered this note—"

"Not quite a lady. The accent gives them away. She was dressed up well enough—a black bonnet and mantle. She wore her hair in a knob at the back. She was tall, well built, had a veil drawn over her face. I tried to detain her, but she was in a rush to get away. She had a hired cab waiting at the door. She seemed frightened, like."

"What time did she come?"

"Not long after you left, madam. I told her you were at the theater and wouldn't be home for some time."

"I see. That will be all, Black. Make sure everything is locked," she said, with a frightened look around her. So many doors and windows to let in an attacker. She went upstairs.

The note, while offering hope, filled her with apprehension. The redheaded woman said she must go alone to Hyde Park. That was full of potential troubles, not least of which was that Luten would not want her to go alone. But if he came along, the woman wouldn't show herself. Was that why she hadn't kept the appointment at the Green Man, because she had been watching from some concealed spot and seen Luten? Odd she didn't mention it. Perhaps she hadn't written that first note that came with the pearl. But if not her, then who?

As Corinne lay in bed, the note clasped between her fingers, she pondered the situation. Luten thought the redhead was in league with Robinson, but Luten had been wrong about Harry. It was possible the redhead was in league with Robinson's murderer. She might even *be* Robinson's murderer. He wouldn't suspect trouble from a woman. His lover could easily get close enough to shoot him. No special strength was required. Was she in league with the Frenchies? She could have hired them. Some of them were close to destitute. She might even be French. But the note was in good English.

On the other hand, if she was innocent, the murderer might have read the notice in the journals and sent this letter. A redheaded woman had delivered it, but it could be anyone, even a man in a wig. Black had mentioned she was tall. The veil had hidden her face. This could be a trap to lure her to her death. The murderer might be hiding behind a tree with a gun aimed at her.

But no, a murderer wouldn't choose such a public place in broad daylight. He'd choose some dark alley, late at night. Hyde Park at noon suggested a frightened woman—the redhead herself. If she really was Robinson's friend, she ought to be warned that she was in danger. If this note was genuine, she already knew it. She was frightened, and she was taking precautions.

Someone must know Robinson's friend, know where she lived. Corinne wished she had tried to find her sooner. She had let Luten sway her, making her think the redhead was of no importance. If she could only call on her before twelve noon, accompanied by an escort—but to discover where she lived would require help. She couldn't go alone to a place like Shepherd's Market to make enquiries. Her first thought was of Luten. He'd insist on going alone, and Corinne felt it was her place to be there.

Coffen was more biddable. She'd ask Coffen's assistance. With that settled, she put the note under her pillow and extinguished her lamp. She was dead tired, but her mind was too overwrought to let her rest. She thought of Harry. Now *he* would gladly help her. He was twice as sharp as Coffen. Of course she wouldn't mention the pearls to Harry. She would claim the woman was a modiste, a virtual wizard with the needle whom she must have make a gown for her, and she had lost the address. Finally, she slept.

Luten called at nine the next morning. Corinne had just finished what she was calling breakfast these days—two cups of coffee. She sat in her Green Saloon, staring at the note that she now knew by heart, trying to decide how to get in touch with Harry. She disliked to go to Grosvenor Square. After the theater invitation, the deCoventrys would be sure she was dangling after him. Yet if she invited him here, Luten might see him and come over. When she recognized Luten's voice at the door, she stuck the note into a copy of Byron's *Childe Harold* on the sofa table and arranged a face to meet him.

He entered smiling. After one glance, the smile faded. "What's the matter?" he asked, hurrying forward.

"Nothing," she said, forcing a smile. She spoke on rapidly to cover her nervousness. "Or rather, everything. I'm brooding about all this business."

He took up a seat beside her, seized her hand and squeezed her fingers. "It will soon be over, my dear. Now, down to business. I want to discuss money with you. If we can't find the pearls, you'll have to hand ten thousand over to deCoventry. I can lend you—"

"No! No, that won't be necessary."

"It would be a loan."

"I'd prefer to sell some of my jewelry," she said stiffly.

Luten was neither surprised nor offended. He was well acquainted with her demmed Irish pride.

"Loans have to be repaid," she continued, "and I live up to my income. I'd have to stint on everything. I shall hold on to my real estate—as you suggested," she threw in, to please him. "I shall sell my diamonds, but thank you for the offer."

"A wise move. Well, we had best get at it. Time is running short. Shall we take them around to a few shops this morning?"

She began to see a way to keep Luten occupied while she arranged with Harry to look for the redhead, and perhaps even while she went to Hyde Park.

"It's so embarrassing," she said, with a pleading look.

"I'll handle it for you," he offered at once. She felt guilty for fooling him when he was so helpful.

"Would you mind?" she asked, in a small voice, gazing at him with her big green eyes, darkened with shadows.

"A pleasure. And I'll speak to Townsend as well. He might have come up with something. The case is not hopeless by any means."

"Oh no. I have not given up," she assured him.

"I see your advertisement is in the journals. I expect you'll remain at home in hope of a reply?"

She already knew it had been in yesterday's papers, where the redheaded woman had presumably seen it. She didn't want to lie, so she just smiled.

Luten spoke on bracingly. "Townsend will have read every scrap of paper in Robinson's house. I made only a cursory look. It's entirely possible he's found something. I'll keep at it all morning and call back around four. We shall go for a drive, as the day is so fine. You really ought to get out, you know." His voice softened to intimacy. "You are losing your glow."

"Thank you for not saying my looks."

Luten scrutinized her closely. No, she had certainly not lost her looks, nor her attraction. The aura of damsel in distress added grace to her charms. "Never. I have no doubt white hair will become you admirably."

She took his hand. "How kind you are to me, dear Luten."

His hands moved forward, as if he would pull her into his arms, but this wasn't the time for lovemaking. "Wait until I've succeeded, before you lavish praise. Then you may dump the whole butter boat on me."

When Corinne went to get her diamonds, Mrs. Ballard was just coming downstairs to breakfast. She reminded her mistress that she planned to attend a card game that evening, if it would not be inconvenient. The dame tended to babble on. Corinne said it would be fine, and went off to fetch the diamonds.

When she had handed them to him, he said, "*Au revoir*, my dear." He tucked the jewelry box into his pocket, placed a fleeting kiss on her cheek and left, feeling like a knight in shining armor.

Corinne wrote to Harry, asking him to call as soon as possible, and sent the note off with a footman in her own carriage, to facilitate his coming. Lord Harry was no early riser and didn't come until ten-thirty. He was mystified by her summons.

"I hope you ain't dangling after me, Corrie," he said. "The dashed butler announced 'A note from Lady deCoventry,' when he handed it to me. Mama heard, of course. She sends her respects, by the by. Is this some clever stunt to get her off your back? Leaving the refusal up to me?"

"Don't count your chickens, cawker! I only want you to do something for me."

"What is it, then?" he asked impatiently.

She told the tale about looking for the redheaded modiste who was a friend of Robinson.

"Doesn't she have a shop?" he asked.

161

"She works out of her home. I heard of her from Lady deLieven. She's all the crack this season. I've forgotten the address, but I know she's a friend of a Mr. Robinson, a carpenter in Shepherd's Market."

He looked at her sharply. "Robinson? He'll not be there, nor will she. He was murdered the other day. I heard Papa and Gaviston discussing it. Bound to happen sooner or later, in his line of work. He used to do dirty work for the honorable members, it seems."

Corinne expressed the proper degree of shock, then continued. "Some of Robinson's neighbors might know who she is, and where she can be reached."

"Sounds like hunting mares' nests, but I am in your debt."

"This will cancel the debt," she said. "And Harry, I'm in a great hurry. Be sure you are back well before noon."

"What's the rush? It's only a gown." He rose to go, then stopped and directed a bright gaze at her. "Isn't it?"

"Perhaps it's a little more than that," she admitted. "It's very important, Harry. Now please go."

She spent the interval during his absence pacing and worrying. Lord Harry returned at eleven-thirty.

"If Robinson had a lady bird, none of his neighbors was aware of it. He didn't do his courting at his shop," he said.

Her spirits sank. "You learned nothing?"

"A stationer who lived nearby said he had seen Robinson and a woman go into the place once or twice late at night, but he couldn't tell what she looked like, and had no idea who she might be. I'm sorry." His intelligent eyes studied her as he spoke. "This has nothing to do with a gown, has it, Corrie?"

She didn't bother to deny it. Harry knew her too well. "No, I'm to meet the woman at Hyde Park at noon— alone. I know nothing about her. I was just trying to discover who she is."

"If you're frightened, don't go. Why the deuce should you?" He realized Corrie wasn't listening. "What does she have on you?" he asked. "She must be holding you to ransom over some indiscretion. I wouldn't pay her a sou, if I were you. She'll only come back for more, and more. Dash it, if you've taken a lover, it's no more than everyone expects. Or is it gambling?"

Corinne completely ignored his question. "Thank you for trying to help me, Harry. I must ask you to leave now."

"I still think you're a fool to pay her."

"It's not a matter of paying. I must speak to her."

Black entered. "It's a quarter to twelve. Your carriage is waiting, milady."

"Let me go with you at least," Harry said.

"No, I must go alone. I shan't be all alone. My coachman will be with me." She didn't tell Harry she was to walk about the park unaccompanied. There could be no danger at high noon.

"I daresay a woman can't harm you." He stopped and frowned. "I say, it has nothing to do with Robinson's death, has it? No, of course not. You didn't even know he was dead."

"Thank you for coming. Sorry I can't offer you a lift."

"You could drop me off at the corner of Piccadilly. It won't take you out of your way."

"Very well."

Once they were in the carriage, Harry saw she was distracted, and didn't try to make conversation. He hopped out at Devonshire House and hailed a passing hackney.

Corinne's carriage continued west on Piccadilly to the corner of Hyde Park. The park was not so busy at the noon hour as it would be later, but Corinne was relieved to see it was by no means deserted. Those present were mostly either youngsters being taken for a romp by their nursemaids or elderly gentlemen strolling at random amongst the trees. A few younger adults walked arm-in-arm and others rode in Rotten Row. Corinne felt conspicuous to walk about unattended. What if some rake or rattle accosted her?

163

At least the day was fine. Sunlight poured from the azure sky, where a breeze sent cotton-wool clouds scudding over treetops. Hundreds of acres of greenery stretched before her.

She headed west toward the Serpentine. Two towheaded youngsters, tended by their nursemaid, were racing toy sailboats on the water. They made an excuse to dawdle a moment. Corinne took up a post beside a mulberry tree and was serenaded by a robin as she waited, looking all around the park. She chanced to glance toward Rotten Row, and saw a woman mounted on a bay mare. The woman had drawn over to the verge and sat still as a statue, staring at her. She was dressed all in black, with a jaunty curled beaver tilted over her eye. As Corinne watched, the woman drew a veil over her face, dismounted and handed the reins to the groom who accompanied her. It was the woman who had been with Robinson at the Pantheon. She had the same statuesque build and same proud carriage. The curls showing beneath her hat glinted coppery in the sunlight.

She looked all around, then began walking toward Corinne. As she drew closer, Corinne, with her heart hammering in her chest, went forward to meet her. They were not more than ten feet apart when the woman suddenly froze in her steps. Her veil concealed her face, but from the angle of her head, she seemed to be looking past Corinne, over her shoulder. Corinne glanced in the same direction, but saw nothing unusual. When she turned back, the woman had turned to leave. She was hastening back to her mount.

"Wait!" Corinne called, hurrying after her. "Please wait!"

Chapter Twenty-one

Corinne called again, "Please wait!"

The woman certainly heard, but she paid no heed. She mounted her bay mare and thundered away, right out of the park. Only then did Corinne take a good look around to see what had frightened her. She saw Lord Luten advancing at a stiff-legged gait.

Vexation at her missed opportunity lent a sharp edge to her voice. "What are you doing here?" she demanded.

"Trying to save your life," he shot back. His fear for her safety changed to anger when he saw she was unharmed. Anger etched lines from his nose to his lips, which were blanched in fury. "What the devil do you think you're doing, coming alone to a place like this? She might have shot you! You lied to me! You said you were staying home." His hands were clenched into fists, as if he meant to strike her.

A shiver of fear trembled up her spine. She had never seen Luten so enraged. At that moment, she could easily believe him capable of murder. She took a faltering step backward.

His hands grabbed her wrists in a vicelike grip that made her bones ache. "You're going home, now, in my carriage," he said, and propelled her by force, protesting every step of the way, to his carriage. He shoved her inside, then went to have a word with his coachman. A footman who had been on the box with the coachman darted off, presumably to have her carriage sent home without her. Her first instinct was to hop out the door, but

165

a second thought told her she would stay behind and read Luten a stiff lecture.

As she sat, waiting, she caught a blur of motion at the corner of her eye. It was a man, to judge by that glimpse of blue jacket. He was slipping behind a tree. A head peeked out. Harry! He grinned, hunched his shoulders, then disappeared again. Had he been worried for her safety, and followed her here?

Before she had time to think, the door opened and Luten got in. He sat on the banquette across from her and the carriage lurched into motion. To keep him from spotting Harry, she began her attack at once. "I do not appreciate being kidnapped in broad daylight, Luten."

"I didn't choose the hour for your folly. As to being kidnapped, I assume you mean rescued."

"Don't be ridiculous. I was merely meeting someone. How did you know I was there?" she asked in a glacial voice.

"I read the note you carelessly left in that book on the sofa table."

"Sunk to reading private correspondence, have you?"

"Only yours, and only at this crucial time. Black showed me the note."

"I shall have a word with Black. You weren't supposed to call until four."

"I changed my mind. I was concerned about you, all alone and worrying," he said, in a voice of heavy sarcasm. "I was unaware that Lord Harry was keeping you company. What did he want?"

Black and his wagging tongue! "A social call," she said airily. There was no need to drag Harry into this.

"As he arrived in your carriage, I assume you sent for him. And he made two visits. I understand he accompanied you when you left home. Even that would have been better than your going alone to meet a dangerous stranger."

"As you took it upon yourself to read my private correspondence, you no doubt noticed the woman asked me to come alone."

"And you, like the veriest greenhead, did it! It was obviously a trap!"

"It was nothing of the sort. If you hadn't come lurching onto the scene to frighten her away, I'd know by now who Robinson was working for. She'll never trust me after this."

"You are hopelessly naive. She didn't mean to help you. At best, she meant to blackmail you into paying for her silence about the pearls."

This had not even occurred to Corinne. Not that it was necessarily the truth. Their disappearance wouldn't be a secret much longer.

"Yes, and Harry killed Rose Grimm. You're not infallible, Luten," she said grandly. "I expect the woman was frightened. Well she might be, if she knows who hired Robinson. The thief has killed everyone else who could help me."

"I would bear that in mind, if I were you, Countess." She directed a cool glance at him. "Did you tell Harry about this?"

"No."

"Thank God for that. What errand did you send him on?"

"Who says I sent him on an errand?"

"Common sense says it. He came, he left, he returned shortly after. What was it—to the bank to get money?"

"I was not being held to ransom!"

He listened, and believed her. She wouldn't be so angry if he had hit on the truth; she'd be wearing her prevaricating face. That face that had made a fool of him in the past. "Just as well. You'll need all you can scrape together to pay deCoventry for the pearls. The highest offer I got for your diamonds was five thousand."

"They're worth twice that!"

"It seems there's a glut of 'em on the market. Five was

the best offer," he said, pleased. She needed his help. He could put restrictions on her freedom, for her own safety.

"You're *enjoying* this," she said, her voice high in disbelief. "I thought you were my friend. I thought you were trying to help me."

"I am." His reply was automatic, given without thinking.

"How very kind, but in future pray limit your help to doing what I ask. I'd have the answer now, if it weren't for you."

"More likely you'd have a bullet through your heart, like Robinson. I wager his redheaded friend did him in. Stole the pearls and made off with them and now plans to sell them to you."

"Would that be before or after she kills me? You're talking utter nonsense, Luten." As an afterthought, she added, "I expect she would have talked to me at the Green Man if you hadn't been there."

"The Green Man was a ruse to get us out of town."

"I don't see any point in that."

Was it possible Luten was right? Robinson's friend had got away with the pearls, and planned to sell them back to her? She couldn't ask the whole price for stolen goods. If she had them, Corinne wanted to get them back.

"Actually, it's possible the woman shot Robinson," Luten continued. "He obviously trusted his murderer. The shot was fired at close range. A woman's dressing gown was found in the clothespress. She was thorough. Townsend didn't find a thing in Robinson's place that could identify her. Not a note, nor a name or address anywhere. Almost as if she had cleaned the place out before leaving." As he spoke, he was halfway to convincing himself the woman was the thief.

"This is all fustian," Corinne said. "Last night you were certain Harry was the culprit."

"He's still a suspect. He might have hired Robinson. Perhaps it was a glimpse of his grinning face that sent the lady scampering, and not myself."

"She couldn't have seen him. He was nowhere near the Serpentine." She came to a guilty stop as she realized what had slipped out. Luten's head turned slowly toward her. His dark eyes bored into hers like a gimlet into soft wood.

"He was there! Where was he hiding?"

"What do you mean?"

"I mean he was there, at the park somewhere. You took him with you."

"I did not! I mercly delivered him to Piccadilly, since I was going that way. You know he has no carriage."

"I know he's desperate for money. Why in God's name did you ask his help, when you have Prance, Pattle and myself?"

"Harry is innocent! Baxter proved that."

"For God's sake, Corinne, use your head. He didn't kill Rose; that doesn't mean he's not involved in the theft."

"This is foolishness," she said with a sniff. "You've done nothing but gone haring off on wild goose chases from the very beginning. If we'd concentrated on the red-head, as I wanted to, I'd have the pearls back by now."

"Well upon my word," Luten exclaimed, stunned by her attack. "That's gratitude for you! I go a mile out of my way, lying to jewelers, rubbing shoulders with actresses and French fortune hunters who claim to be *contes*, illegally entering various establishments, stumbling over corpses and causing some consternation at Bow Street, and this is the thanks I get. If you think you can do better without me, so be it, Countess. You're on your own. Good luck to you."

Luten uttered a bah of disgust, then turned to look out the window, to show he was through with her. The short drive continued in silence. When the carriage stopped on Berkeley Square, Corinne said ironically. "Thank you so much for your *help*, Luten."

Without looking at her, he growled, "Go to hell."

After this remark, she didn't wait for the coachman but

169

opened the door herself and hopped down without benefit of the stairs. She strode into the house and gave Black a Bear Garden jaw for his ill judgment and impertinence in retailing her movements to Luten.

"He asked," was Black's only defense. "He seemed most upset when he read about you going to meet the woman."

Corinne was too upset herself to think straight. She paced to and fro in the saloon, occasionally tossing a cushion. When Black came to the door to see if she would like anything, she accepted a glass of wine and sat down to think, or try to.

She knew she had been abominably rude to Luten, but really it was the outside of enough that he had sent the woman in black running away just when she was within grasp. There wouldn't be another chance. The woman wouldn't answer another appeal. She thought it had been a trap. But why had a glimpse of Luten frightened her so? Or was it—could it possibly have been a glimpse of Harry that sent her off?

The woman knew who Robinson had been working for. The man this woman feared was obviously Robinson's killer. No doubt the killer feared the redheaded woman as well. She could reveal the murderer. She was wise to take no chances. As the image of the woman's frozen posture played in Corinne's mind, she became convinced that the woman had seen the murderer in the park. But who was he? Luten? Harry? Or someone else entirely?

The killer-cum-thief might have read her notice in the journals and followed her in the hope that she'd lead him to the woman in black, as indeed she had. At least the woman had made good her escape. The situation seemed hopeless. The woman would surely flee town now—run for her life.

Corinne's brooding was interrupted by a knock on the door. Black entered and handed her a package. Opening it, she saw the box containing her diamonds. Luten had

170

returned them. He hadn't even bothered to enclose a note. He had washed his hands of her. Her first sharp stab of regret was subdued by anger. And after he had promised he would help her. His lovemaking was no more to be trusted than his promises. She didn't need him.

She looked at the diamonds, sparkling dully in their blue satin nest. How was it possible they were only worth five thousand pounds, when George had paid ten? Still, five thousand was better than nothing. If she sold her bracelet and the ruby ring and that brooch that she never wore, the whole would come to over seven thousand. And she wouldn't have a single piece of jewelry to wear. She might take out a mortgage on the house. A pinched future of scrimping and saving stretched before her. She sipped the wine, scheming how to raise ten thousand pounds without jeopardizing her future. When the door knocker sounded again, she was sure it would be Coffen or Prance. She knew it wouldn't be Luten. Whoever it was, Black didn't show her caller in at once. She could hear Black talking to him.

A moment later, Black walked in and handed her a note. "It's from her," he said importantly.

Corinne was on her feet, darting to the door. "You mean she's here! Why didn't you show her in!" There was no need to further identify "her," when it was said in that significant way.

"Nay, she had it delivered by a linkboy."

"Oh." Corinne returned to her seat.

"I asked him where he got it. Said he was sworn not to tell, but I fed him a glass of wine and chatted a little and found out he just came from New Bond Street. She was in a hired cab."

How had she got rid of her mount and gotten into a cab so quickly? Her groom could have helped her.

"That will be all, Black," she said, and waited until he had taken his reluctant departure before opening the note.

Chapter Twenty-two

Inside the folded note there was an enclosure, written on rich vellum paper. Corinne, eager to get to the cream of the message, set it aside. The woman's note had obviously been written in haste, probably in a moving carriage. Even before Corinne read it, the word Luten leapt off the page to quicken her heartbeat. She hastily scanned the note, to put the name in context.

Dear Lady deCoventry,

On the day of the masquerade, Robinson received the enclosed note from Lord Luten asking him to "steal" your pearls for a prank at the party that night. He said it was a bet, and the pearls were not real ones. Luten told Robinson not to be in touch with him. Robinson did exactly what Lord Luten asked. Robinson was to call on me the next night. When he didn't come, I was worried and went to Shepherd's Market. I saw Luten leaving the shop. When I went inside, I found Robinson dead on the floor.

Robinson told me at the masquerade that he thought the pearls were genuine and gave me Luten's note for safekeeping in case of trouble. He was worried, with good reason. Luten is a thief and a murderer. Stay away from him. Don't try to get in touch with me. I have left London.

It was signed *Mr. Robinson's friend—and yours.*

Corinne read the letter a second time, bewildered and

172

disbelieving. Then she read the enclosed note. It was on Luten's crested stationery, written in his bold fist.

Dear Robinson,

Enclosed please find ten pounds for the following job. Lady deCoventry will be wearing a long strand of faux pearls at my masquerade party at the Pantheon tonight. She will be dressed as Cleopatra. I want you to wear the Robin Hood costume I will send you and steal the pearls. I wore the costume myself at another party, and with luck, she might mistake you for me. Don't contact me there or she will suspect my little trick. Five hundred pounds are riding on a bet that I cannot get the necklace. Ten percent of it is yours if you succeed.

As soon as you have got the necklace, do the following—and try not to be seen—go to Berkeley Square. In Lady deCoventry's backyard there is a lilac bush. Hang the necklace on a lower branch. I will recover it from there and send you your tithe tomorrow. Bonne chance!

Luten.

Corinne sank onto the sofa, staring at the two letters. She couldn't believe what she had just read. It was some trick. But the stationery was Luten's. She had seen it hundreds of times. The handwriting, too, looked exactly like his.

She puzzled over the documents, line by line. Luten had said the pearls were fakes to ensure Robinson's help. Robinson might hesitate to steal genuine pearls, but fake jewelry was of small value. And returning the pearls to her own backyard also added a note of innocence. But why had Luten done it in the first place?

He knew she had to hand the necklace over to deCoventry in a few days. He must have realized how worried she would be. There had been no bet. That, too, was to ensure Robinson's compliance. She could only conclude Luten had stolen them to punish her for having rejected his offer of marriage. He had never really got over it. Those malicious things he said, half in jest, were actually meant to hurt her. The final indignity was to make her love him, to make a fool of her and break her heart.

Did he plan to return the pearls after she had suffered sufficiently? Surely he didn't plan to keep them, to rob her of ten thousand pounds! He was rich as Croesus. But now that the plan had gone wrong, he could hardly give them back without revealing his own involvement.

She stiffened as a new thought occurred to her. Perhaps the pearls were still in the lilac bush! She darted down to the kitchen, out the back door into the little yard. The lilac bush had grown tall. She had to drag a chair over to it to reach the branch. But after a thorough search, she confirmed what she already knew. The pearls were not there.

She returned to the Green Saloon and slumped on the sofa. As she poked and prodded at the various clues, the thing began to fall apart. Luten already possessed a Robin Hood costume; he had no need to get one from Rosie Grimm—unless he meant it to be found. Looking for the costume had been the first thing he suggested after she noticed the pearls were missing and Robin Hood was gone. Surely he was not so determined to show herself a lesson that he would murder two innocent people to accomplish it. Yet there was the letter, written in his hand, on his stationery.

It must have started out as a prank, and something had gone dreadfully wrong somewhere along the way. The redheaded woman's letter said Robinson thought the pearls were genuine. Had he confronted Luten with his knowledge, and in an argument, had Luten shot Robinson? That would explain Luten's vexation at her going to meet the redheaded woman, and his eagerness to prevent it. He wasn't concerned for her safety, but for his own.

But even before Robinson's murder, Rosie Grimm had been strangled. Corinne couldn't see Luten carrying on with a seamstress. His occasional mistresses were not lowborn young girls but society matrons or the higher class of lightskirt. And besides, he wouldn't have gone to Rose to enquire about the costume if she was acquainted with him—unless it was all an act. Rose was not a subtle girl; she would have let something slip. Going to Drury Lane had been Luten's idea, hadn't it?

She conned the woman's letter again. Robinson, she noticed, had received the letter from Luten. Luten hadn't gone in person. A man didn't put his name to something in writing if he feared the consequences. Luten would have gone in person if he had been planning actually to steal the pearls. The whole transaction, including the extra payment after the theft, was to be done by post. The logical explanation was that someone had forged the letter and signed Luten's name.

If that was true, then Luten had been right about one thing. Someone had wished to involve him from the beginning. That was why he had chosen a Robin Hood costume. It was odd the writer hadn't asked Robinson to keep mum about the intrigue. He had only asked him not to approach Luten. That looked suspicious. He didn't care if Robinson mentioned it to a friend or two. Perhaps he wanted him to bruit Luten's name about, but not to confront Luten in person. As no mention of Luten had surfaced until now, it seemed the only one Robinson had told was the redheaded woman. No wonder she ran for her life when she saw Luten running toward her at Hyde Park!

Who had delivered the note and the costume to Robinson? How could they find that out, now that Robinson was dead? In any case, it had probably been an anonymous linkboy who would never be found.

A half hour passed while Corinne sat, deep in thought.

She should tell Luten. But when she looked at the letter that looked so very much like his handwriting, she hesitated. What if he *had* written this note? Two people had been killed already. But when she remembered Rose Grimm, she refused to believe Luten had done that. Finally, Corinne decided to discuss the matter with her oldest and best friend, Coffen Pattle. She asked Black to send a footboy over to his house and ask him to call.

He came within minutes. "I fear I have no good news for you," he said. "I've been keeping my ears open but come up dry as a bone."

"I heard from the redheaded woman," she said, and relayed her activities, omitting nothing.

"Harry, eh? I wonder if it was a whiff of young Harry that sent her galloping off," was Coffen's speech at the end of her story. "You haven't forgotten Harry was visiting de Creuse yesterday."

"We know why he was there. DeCoventry sent him."

Coffen nodded, satisfied. "It wouldn't be the first time he's had Gaviston or Harry hint ineligible suitors away."

"I was wondering if it might have been a whiff of Luten that set her off," she said, handing him the letters. "I received these half an hour ago."

As he read them, a deep frown settled between his brows. He studied the note ostensibly from Luten closely, then sat staring into space, while Corinne waited for his reaction.

"How the devil did the bounder get hold of Luten's letter paper?" was his first speech.

"You think it's a forgery, then?"

He stared as if she were a Bedlamite. "Surely you're not suggesting Luten wrote this?"

"It does look like his writing, and it's his paper."

"That's the point of a forgery, Corinne. It's someone who knows his fist, and knows him well enough to have been in his house and pocketed the paper. Use your head. Luten talked to Baxter half a dozen times. Baxter would have run him through if he was Rose's beau. Maybe the redhead did recognize Luten. Mean to say, his name is on the forged letter. *She* thinks he did it, since she don't know him. Very likely that's what set her off. The thing to do, we'll show these letters to Luten and hear what he has to say for himself."

Before Corinne replied, the knocker sounded again.

It was Sir Reginald Prance. "What is afoot, folks?" he asked, strolling in and peering at them through his raised quizzing glass. "I feel as if I'd interrupted a seduction. Will someone please *say* something!"

"Cast your peepers on these letters," Coffen said, handing them to him.

"First I should tell you where they came from," Corinne said, and gave him a brief outline of her day.

"Aren't you the busy little bee!" was his only comment before lifting his coattails and sitting down to peruse the papers. When he was done, he exhaled a loud breath, and sat, stunned to momentary silence.

"One hardly knows whether to laugh or be angry. The bald-faced gall of whoever is responsible for this jape quite takes the breath away. And the writing, too, so very like Luten's. I shall warn Luten to check with his bank to make sure this fellow ain't forging checks on his account."

"There, I told you so," Coffen said to Corinne.

Prance turned a mischievous eye on her. "You cannot mean you thought Luten . . . There is a facer for him. It would add a delightful twist to the tangled web if Luten had written the letter, but it is not possible. It would necessitate Luten's carrying on with Rose Grimm, and while I can envisage him murdering Robinson if the situation warranted, I cannot see him creeping up the stairs of a decrepit rooming house to throw himself on a seamstress. That is not Luten. I acquit him."

Coffen nodded. "No need to ask if you had a look in the lilac bush, Corrie?"

"I did. The necklace isn't there."

"No clues?"

"No."

"Thing to do, then, show these letters to Luten, see what he has to say."

"By all means," Prance said. He turned to Corinne and added, "A word to the wise, my beloved. I would not intimate to Luten that you harbored a single doubt as to his innocence. He might take a pet. Luten in one of his pets is not a pretty sight."

"I'm not going with you," she said. "I've already seen Luten in one of his pets today. That I let you show him the letters tells him I don't believe he is guilty."

"But it will be utterly amusing, dear heart!" Prance exclaimed. "You will not want to miss all the fun of figuring out who wrote this, and what must be done about it."

Pride prevented her from accepting. "I've had enough excitement today. You will let me know if you come to any conclusions?"

"I personally undertake to keep you fully informed, even if you did not see fit to share this treasure trove with me," he said with a moue. "Had I not spotted Coffen darting to your door and come over, I would have missed this tremendous development. That was infinitely mean of you, Countess. You know I thrive on drama."

"Then you must be thriving to your heart's content today," Coffen said, and heaved himself up from the sofa. "We'll come back to tell you what Luten says, Corinne."

"Thank you," she said in a weak voice.

When she was alone, she continued thinking over the situation. Prance and Coffen had known Luten from the egg, and they could not even entertain the possibility that he was guilty, so very likely he wasn't. She had told him his help was no longer wanted, but she knew he would pitch himself back into the fray now that his own reputation was involved.

She remembered Luten's proposal, years ago, and his shock, quickly turning to anger, when she refused. She had never told anyone of his proposal. Not even Coffen or Sir Reggie. And apparently Luten hadn't either, since neither of them ever mentioned it. His pride had kept the secret sealed in his breast. Had it festered there, waiting all this time to find revenge? She had seen a side of him his closest friends had never seen. Relationships were different between men and women than between members of the same sex. They were more violent, more passionate in both love and hate. Yet the other night his tenderness had seemed sincere.

What if Luten *had* written that letter? Not for the sake of stealing her pearls, but just to have his revenge on her. He tried to conceal it, but he had been pleased when he told her the diamonds were only worth five thousand. What if all his so-called help was nothing else but an effort to keep her from learning the truth? It was more important than ever to find the woman in black. And Corinne hadn't the least idea where to begin looking, now that she had left London.

Chapter Twenty-three

Corinne kept a watch on Luten's front door from her saloon, expecting every moment to see the three gentlemen come striding across the street to discuss matters with her. After half an hour's waiting, she decided Luten was still angry with her. At that time, Mrs. Ballard returned from the circulating library with a friend and Corinne had to leave the window to take tea with them. Mrs. Crosby was a good gossiper. Tea lasted over an hour. After she had left, Black told his mistress the three gentlemen left together in his lordship's hunting carriage an hour ago.

Corinne assumed they were off trying to discover who had forged the letter, or delivered it, or something. The afternoon dragged on with no word from them. While waiting for dinner, she told Mrs. Ballard what had been going forth during her absence.

Mrs. Ballard, who was frightened of her own shadow, hardly knew what to make of such nefarious goings-on, but like the others, she was firmly on Luten's side.

"It is the work of the Tories to discredit him," was her conclusion. "That study on the rotten boroughs he is working up displeases a number of Tories."

"I think it's a more personal matter," Corinne replied. "What interests me more is how I can find the redheaded woman. I can hardly place advertisements in all the small local journals. There are hundreds of them. If I could figure out where she might have gone to hide herself—"

"Did she not have family? Would she have gone to them?"

"I don't know. Lady deLieven might be able to tell me. She seemed to have some familiarity with Robinson. I'll write to her now. At least it will be something to do."

"I shall have a lie-down before dinner. You don't plan to go out this evening, dear?"

"No, I expect to be at home, waiting." Waiting for what?

"Your jonquil gown will be good enough, then. You haven't forgotten I'm promised for a few hands of whist and some scandal broth this evening? I shan't be late."

"That's quite all right."

"Come with me. I don't like to leave you home alone."

"No, I must be here. You go ahead."

"If you're sure you don't mind."

By dinnertime, Corinne had written to Lady deLieven and had a reply. "I have no knowledge of Robinson's lady friend, as I told Luten." Luten had been there before her. There was still no word from him, nor had Prance informed her what was going forth, as he had promised he would. When she came down to dinner, she had a word with Black. "Have the gentlemen returned yet, Black?" she asked.

"I've not seen them, and I've kept a pretty sharp eye on the road," Black replied. "I'll slip across the street and have a word with his lordship's butler if you like."

"Don't bother. If Luten has decided to keep me in the dark, he will have told his butler to keep mum."

"And Evans will never disobey. He's faithful as a dog. As we all are, milady," he added with an ingratiating smile. "I'll let you know when they return."

Dinner was a desultory affair. Corinne took two spoonfuls of soup and pushed a piece of cod around her plate. She could think of nothing but those letters, which she wouldn't discuss in front of the servants, so instead Mrs. Ballard told her the entire plot of a novel Mrs. Crosby had recommended to her. Mrs. Ballard had been told as a girl that it was a lady's duty to keep the conversation going on polite subjects, especially at the dinner table. It was a duty she seldom had to perform. There was not usually any lack of conversation at the countess's board.

"You must read it, milady," she finished, after she had revealed all the story's secrets.

"It sounds lovely," Corinne said. She hadn't heard a word.

"I like an edifying story, where wrongdoing is punished, as it should be. I shall enjoy reading *The Vicar of Wakefield*."

Mrs. Ballard did not keep late hours. She left the house immediately after dinner, promising to be home not later than twelve. Five minutes after she left, Corinne finally received word from Luten. Black brought a note to her, where she sat alone in the Green Saloon, staring into the cold grate as intently as if she were watching the play of flames. But what she saw in her mind's eye was that Luten had forsaken her. She could bear the rest if it weren't for that.

"This just came for you from his lordship, milady," Black said, handing her the note. It had been folded once and sealed with a gold wafer. "He's not been home. P'raps he sent it from Whitehall. It wasn't one of his lordship's footmen who brought it, but a young fellow in a hackney cab."

"Thank you." She snatched the letter eagerly, surprised that Luten had gone to the House, but perhaps his investigations had led him there. She opened the note and read a brief message.

Dear Countess,

She was sunk to countess again.

I have got a line on the mysterious woman. She won't talk to me, but says she will tell you what you want to

182

*know. She will not go to Berkeley Square, as she fears
she is being followed. You are to come alone in a
hackney cab at once to her apartment at 10 Mercer
Street, two houses off Long Acre, on the west side. She
does not want your carriage recognized standing at
her door. I will meet you there and take you home
after. Your troubles will soon be over, Countess.*

Your faithful servant, Luten.

"Is it good news or bad?" Black enquired, when she
lowered the note.

"Oh, good news. Excellent," she replied, but Black
knew that when his beloved bit into her lower lip with
her little white teeth, she was worried, as indeed she was.

To go alone at night to Long Acre was a daunting
prospect. Yet she was, of course, happy to read that
Luten had found the redheaded woman, and that she had
agreed to talk. What caused a doubt was the earlier
forgery, also in Luten's hand, and the woman's first letter
stating that she was leaving London at once. Perhaps she
had meant as soon as she could arrange it. Naturally
she'd have to pack her belongings and arrange transportation. One could not just walk away from one's
home without settling the domestic details. "She won't
talk to me" had the ring of truth to it at least. Perhaps the
meeting had been arranged through Prance or Coffen.
Since it was vitally necessary to see the woman, Corinne
felt she must take the chance.

"Send Jackie out to find me a hackney, Black," she said.

"Your own rig will be back within half an hour. Mrs.
Ballard has only gone to Grosvenor Square."

"The note says I am to take a hired carriage."

His fierce eyebrows snapped together. "Where to?" he
demanded.

"Long Acre," she said, staring at him fearfully.

"Not alone you're not!" he declared. Black felt

183

protective toward his young mistress, and occasionally forgot himself.

"Luten will meet me there and drive me home," she said.

"Is that what the note says?"

"Yes." She hesitated a moment, then gave Black the note. She wanted another opinion on it, and trusted Black.

"It looks like his hand," Black said doubtfully. He was aware of the other spurious note attributed to Luten, after eavesdropping on her discussion with Pattle and Sir Reginald.

"I could send a footman over just to see that Luten is not at home," she said. "I would look a fool to go darting off without checking, after what has been going on."

At this critical juncture, there was no pretending that Black was unaware of matters. "You stole the words right out of my mouth," he said. He summoned Jackie, who darted across the road to Luten's house. He was back within a minute.

"His lordship hasn't been home for hours," Jackie reported. "They don't know where he is, milady."

"I fancy we do," Black said. "That's all, lad. Take care of my front door for me for a minute. Her ladyship and I are having a private word." Jackie left.

"I expect Luten wrote this note from Whitehall," the countess said, looking uncertainly at it.

"Or his club. About this trip, milady, why don't I go along with you? I could hire a rig in two shakes of a dog's tail and drive it myself. It'll only cost a guinea to hire the rig and nags for a couple of hours."

She liked the idea of having someone she trusted with her. "Very well. Thank you, Black. I appreciate your help." She picked up her reticule and handed him two guineas.

Black's fawning smile had more to do with her trusting him than the guinea tip. The countess featured strongly in Black's inner romantic life. His mistress filled not only his daily hours but his dreams as well. In his dreams, he was not Black, the butler, but Lord Blackwell, the master of Blackwell Hall.

"Of course you'll take a pistol," he said, with a commanding look.

"An excellent idea, Black. Now where is my pistol—"

"Bottom drawer of the study desk. I'll get it."

They parted, Corinne to don her pelisse and bonnet, and Black to get the pistol, then run down to the corner of Piccadilly and bribe a hackney driver to lend him his carriage and nag. He borrowed the man's hat as well. There was no duplicating a hackney driver's hat. The decrepitude of that particular article was only achieved by years of exposure to sun, wind, dust, rain, sleet and snow.

Within twenty minutes of receiving the note, the countess was being shown into a shabby but once-elegant carriage formerly owned by Lord Eldon. The crest was beginning to show through the fading black paint on the door panel. Once alone inside the carriage, rattling along through the shadows, a hundred worries and fears assailed her. What if the note was another forgery? She removed the pistol from her reticule to the pocket of her pelisse, for easier access. Traffic was brisk as the carriage proceeded east along Piccadilly, past tall houses, clubs and hotels. As they neared Haymarket, the Haymarket nuns began to appear, blowzy women in garish gowns, flaunting their wares in hopes of enticing a customer.

When they passed into Long Acre, the carriages were fewer, the pedestrians more frequent and the prostitutes more shabby. Corinne did not have to traverse the worst part of Long Acre, as she had feared. She spotted a sign proclaiming Mercer Street a block before they came to Covent Garden theater.

The carriage turned left into Mercer Street, where tall houses huddled close together. The note said two houses off Long Acre, on the west side of the street. The carriage drew to a stop in front of a tall brown brick building, once the private residence of an ambitious merchant. It looked down on its neighbors as it shouldered its way a story above them. Lights showed at several of the windows.

Black appeared at the door to help her down. "I'll drive around the corner and circle back. Any sign of his lordship?"

She looked to the doorway of the house. It opened, and a tall gentleman peered out. The proud angle of his head and the wide shoulders told her it was Luten. She breathed more easily.

"Yes, there he is. I wasn't sure he'd actually be here. He said he would drive me home after."

"I'll wait, just in case."

"How can I ever thank you, Black?"

"I'll be nearby if you need me. Off you go, then." This was as close as reality was likely to come to his dreams, and he added daringly, "Take care of yourself, milady. I wouldn't want anything to happen to you." Not the usual "we," including all her servants, but "I," Lord Blackwell, master of Blackwell Hall.

Some impulse, she hardly knew what caused it, perhaps it was no more than the urge to touch another human being, made the countess lean over and place a grateful kiss on Black's swarthy cheek. His mouth fell open, his hand flew to the cherished inch of flesh. Beyond words, he just stood gaping after her as she went up the walk to meet Lord Luten.

"Luten!" she said, hurrying through the shadows.

A hand came out to greet her. Not Luten's hand. It was bigger, less shapely. It closed tightly over her fingers. She looked up, and saw Gaviston's smiling face looming above her.

"Gaviston! What are you doing here?"

"Good evening, Cuz," he said, in a strangely gloating voice. "I see you got the message. Come in. Come in." He drew her into the hallway and closed the door.

Chapter Twenty-four

"It's certainly my letter paper," Luten said, examining the note that Prance had so gleefully given him. "The writing is similar, but I don't sign my name with such a flourishing *L*. The folks who read handwriting tell us that is a sign of a well-developed ego."

"I thought the *L* quite like yours!" Prance murmured. "Have you any notion who did it?"

"Someone who doesn't love me," Luten replied with a shrug. "That hardly limits the field. Mouldy and Company for starters. No, the question is *cui bono*?"

"An actress, is she?" Coffen asked. "Why don't I know the name?"

"Because you're ignorant as a swan, Coffen," Prance explained. "It's Latin. Who benefits from the theft of the pearls? And before you further display your astonishing ignorance, pray do not say 'the thief.' "

"I wasn't going to."

"The pearls are the heart of the matter," Luten announced. "And no one is involved in their disposition except the deCoventrys and Corinne."

"The theft was no *kooey bono* to Corinne," Coffen said.

"One could argue otherwise," Luten replied, winning two rebukeful looks. "Strictly in the way of covering all possible candidates. She was loath to give them to their rightful owner. She might have arranged the theft and thrown herself on deCoventry's mercy, but I can't believe she turned murderer to prevent discovery of her

187

stunt. If Harry is innocent—I say if—there remains only deCoventry *père* and elder *fils*, Gaviston."

"Rubbish. Corinne was to give the pearls to deCoventry on Friday," Coffen said.

"That is precisely why they were stolen: because the originals had been sold and a duplicate necklace put in their place."

"That again!" Coffen scoffed.

"No, still. One large, genuine pearl is not hard to come by. It threw us off the scent entirely. We wasted a day at the Green Man, while Harry consorted with the French *contes*."

"Or it could be Gaviston," Prance said.

"He could have snatched a sheet of my stationery from my office at Westminster as easily as Harry could have done from my study," Luten said. "Easier. I keep a supply of personal note paper there. Gaviston has visited my office a few times recently, inexplicably pestering me about some Austrian question I have nothing to do with. He knows my writing."

"I don't see Gaviston being mixed up in anything like this," Coffen said. "He's next door to a Methodist."

"Almost too revoltingly good to believe," Prance said, lifting an eyebrow in question. "But with an eye for the ladies. No one is all sweetness and light. That strain of original sin—one assumes it was sexual in nature—will find some outlet. Ladies fall in love with their priests, and prudes like Gaviston with lightskirts. He dropped his mistress a month ago when he took up with Lady Angela. Two weeks ago, Rose Grimm found herself a new beau. Just about the time Gaviston would be developing horn fever. To ensure privacy, he gave Rose a false name—and nationality. Gaviston is nothing if not thorough. And he speaks French fluently."

"I thought it was German he spoke," Coffen mentioned.

Luten wore a pensive look. "That too. He was assigned to Austria as so few of Castlereagh's men speak German."

"Baxter said *M'sewer* looked like a cold fish," Coffen

said, tugging at his ear. "That ought to have given us the clue right there. But didn't Baxter say *M'sewer* was old?"

"Not old; older than Harry," Prance said. "He didn't mention gray hair, for instance. Gaviston is a decade older than Harry, and his pompous air adds another decade."

"Thing to do," Coffen said, "haul Baxter along to the House to have a look at Gaviston."

"It's possible Gaviston got into Corinne's safe to make the switch while Harry was living at her house," Prance said, "but why would he need the money? He has a handsome allowance. He lives an ordered life. He doesn't gamble."

"Ladies are always a gamble," Luten said. "If you were a lady, wouldn't you set a high price to sell your favors to Gaviston?"

"There's not enough money in the mint to make me do it."

"There you are, then," Luten continued. "He fancied himself enamored of that opera singer he was seeing and needed the blunt to keep her happy, or at least satisfied."

"Let's go pick up Baxter," Coffen said, rising.

"I'll take him up to the visitors' gallery and ask him to scan the honorable members," Luten said, also rising. "But before I pick up Baxter, I'll stop and see if Gaviston is in the House today."

The three gentlemen left in Luten's carriage. At the House of Lords, Luten said, "I'll go in alone. No point alarming Gaviston by all of us rushing in. He might make a run for it."

He asked a page boy to take a look into the Upper House and tell him if Lord Gaviston was there.

"I can tell you he isn't," the young fellow replied. "He stopped by early this morning. Said he had a report to write and needed peace and quiet. He took a dispatch box home to work there."

Luten flipped a coin to the page. "Thank you," he said, and returned to his carriage.

"He hasn't been there since early this morning," he said to the others. "Took work home to do. I'd give a monkey to know what he's up to."

"We know what he was up to," Coffen said. "That letter he sent Corinne—stands to reason he read her notice in the journal and has been keeping an eye on her. Probably followed her to Hyde Park and saw the redhead shab off before Corinne spoke to her."

Prance and Luten exchanged a questioning look. "He might be right," Prance said uncertainly. "If he saw the second letter arrive, he must be worried."

"He could hardly lurk in the bushes like a hedgebird," Luten said. "Someone would have seen him. If he really was at home, Harry might have told him Corinne went to see the woman."

"That's more like it," Prance said. "I fancy Corinne told him not to tell, but Harry has no notion of discretion."

"How did he get your writing paper if he wasn't at the House?" Coffen asked.

"He might have taken it any time," Luten replied. "He had already used it to write to Robinson."

"Thorough." Coffen nodded. "So, what do we do? One of us calls for him at Grosvenor Square to see if he's home, before we take Baxter along?"

Luten said, "I'll go. If he's home, I might lure him out on the pretext that Castlereagh requires his assistance in that Austrian crisis. I'll drop you off at Brook's and pick you up there."

"Suits me. I could do with a wet," Coffen said.

While they awaited Luten's return at Brook's, Prance said, "I told Corinne I'd keep her informed. I should send her a message. The poor girl is on nettles."

"We'll soon be able to tell her her troubles are over. You like the grand gesture, Prance."

"True. It will be a divine moment, when the tears of gratitude sprout in her emerald eyes."

"It ain't you she'll be sprouting at. It'll be Luten."

"If he's right," Prance added.

"You think he ain't?"

"Stop chattering, Pattle. I'm trying to overhear what Lamb is saying. His wife produces such luscious scandal. London would be barren without it. Since the shattering of the Devonshire *ménage à trois*, Caro Lamb and Byron are all that keep us in gossip."

Pattle and Prance played a desultory hand of cards to pass the time until Luten returned. His anxious face told them something was amiss, even before he spoke. "He's not at home," Luten said. "I was told he left at nine this morning for Whitehall and didn't return."

"By Jove, he's been kidnapped!" Coffen exclaimed.

"No, Coffen," Prance said. "It's a ruse. He is afoot in London, looking for the redheaded woman to silence her."

"Ah, just so." Coffen nodded. "Thing to do, find her before he does. If he hasn't already."

Prance said, "Her note said she was leaving town immediately, *n'est-ce pas*?"

"Gaviston hasn't read her note," Coffen pointed out.

"How utterly demoralizing. You are right—again. I believe Gaviston's looking for her. If we find where she lives, I expect we'll find him. But where to look? London is so monstrous. She doesn't live in a vacuum. She must buy food and gowns and bonnets, hire horses occasionally."

"She wouldn't live in the west end," Coffen said. "She ain't a lady, yet she's a touch above Long Acre. Somewhere near Robinson? I mean to say, how else did she meet him?"

"We'll start there," Luten said. "Fan out and cover every milliner and modiste and greengrocer in that area. We'll meet at Robinson's place in an hour to compare notes."

"A tall redhead" wasn't much to go on, but they drove to Shepherd's Market to begin touring the area. When they met an hour later, none of them had discovered anything.

"I don't think she lived anywhere near here," Prance said. "Where the lightskirts of her class often live is in the theater district. She might even have been an actress."

"No," Coffen said. "I'd know her if she was. I don't."

"*Before* you became a walking encyclopedia of the female dramatis personae, I mean. I shouldn't be surprised if Robinson met her in the Green Room."

"Might have been before my time," Coffen agreed. "Don't know about you lot, but I'm ready for fork work. Shall we peck a bite?"

"We'll drive to the theater district and make enquiries at the shops," Luten said.

"Fasting is good for the soul, to say nothing of the figure," Prance said to Coffen.

"You mean we ain't getting any lunch, in other words. Where do we meet for dinner?"

"Brook's," Luten said.

Coffen went, grumbling, to the carriage.

While Luten and Prance searched the theater district, Coffen nipped into Covent Garden for a glass of wine and a biscuit in the Green Room, and to ask some questions. At this hour, the women there were either past their prime or young girls just beginning their careers. Coffen approached an older woman. There had been a certain maturity in the redhead's physique.

"It's Sally Glass, isn't it?" he said.

A woman with so much rouge stuccoed on her cheeks that they looked like the sides of a house opened her lips in a delighted smile. "You remember me!" she exclaimed.

He only knew her name, but he was kind. "I'll never forget the first time I saw you on the stage," he said.

"Go on. A pup like you don't remember me."

"How could I forget that voice? Tell me, Sally," he said, getting right down to business, "do you remember an actress—a big woman like yourself. Well built," he added hastily. "Red hair. Left the theater awhile back. A fellow named Robinson—"

"That's Lily McGee you mean. I remember her well. We toured Yorkshire together two decades ago. I haven't seen her in an age. I heard Robinson was kilt. Isn't that a caution? I'd ought to go to visit Lily."

Coffen quivered like a pointer who has caught the scent. "You know where she lives?"

"Of course I do. We only live two blocks apart."

"Where? Exactly where?"

"On Macklin Street, off Drury Lane, halfway between Long Acre and High Holborn. Lily's place is on the right-hand corner just off Drury Lane. She has the top floor. Madam Labarre, the fortune teller, has the bottom."

"I'm obliged to you, Sally. Here's a little something for your trouble." He handed her a half crown and tore off. Sally put the coin between her teeth to test its authenticity. Satisfied that it was genuine, she smiled at it, slid it into her reticule and picked up another glass of wine.

Outside the theater, Coffen stood a moment, turning this way and that. He felt it his duty to share his stunning discovery with his friends. He began a tour of the streets, peering in at windows and making enquiries. When he had been searching for an hour, he began to fear he'd taken the wrong course. He ought to have darted straight to Macklin Street. He'd do it now, as soon as he could find his way there.

Since his feet were killing him, he decided to hire a hackney—try to find one in this godforsaken part of town! Eventually he spotted one and went running after it to be driven to Macklin Street. He looked for his friends as he went. He had still not seen them when the hackney drew to a stop in front of a gray brick house on the designated corner. It was slightly larger than the dovecote on his country estate. Not exactly a hovel, but he would have thought Robinson would do better by Lily.

"Wait for me," he told the driver, and got out.

"I'll take my blunt now, if you don't mind, sir." The man's open palm reached under Coffen's nose.

"Dash it, I said wait for me."

"And I said pay up, mister," the driver said belligerently. "Houses have back doors, don't they?"

"Of course they have, and roofs too. What's that to do with anything?"

As the outstretched hand was clenching into a fist, Coffen paid up. The shadows of evening were fading into darkness. He noticed there were lamps burning in two windows downstairs, none above, which looked as if Lily had either left, or was already lying on the floor, dead as a doorknob. He decided he'd just have a word with Madame Labarre. Ask if Lily was at home, and if she'd had any callers today.

He had to knock three times before the door was answered. For that three-quarters of a minute, he imagined not only Lily but also Madame Labarre lying in a pool of blood. But the door opened at his third knock and a crone with a black shawl over her head beckoned him in with a bony finger. His flesh crawled to look at her. She looked like some witch out of the fairy tales that used to frighten him when he was a tad.

"Ye'll have to wait, melord," she said, with a smile that showed a dim set of teeth. "I'm giving a reading." Her accent bore no trace of France, despite the name.

"I didn't come for a reading. I'm looking for Lily McGee."

"You'll not find her here. Lily is too grand for us now. She's moved uptown, hasn't she?"

"Is that so? I was told I'd find her here."

"She's long gone. Sorry."

The door began to close. He put his fingers around it to stop its movement, doing some damage to his knuckles in the process. "Would you know where she's living now?"

Madame Labarre gave an impatient tsk. "Come back

later. I'm doing a reading. You're interrupting my client. I have an address somewhere about the place."

"I'd be obliged if you could find it," he said, drawing out a shiny golden boy.

Her bony fingers snatched it, like a hawk leaping on its prey. "Ten Mercer Street," she said.

"I thought you had to look it up," he said suspiciously.

The dim teeth appeared again. "It happens another gent was asking for the address recently. I just remembered it."

Coffen didn't smile, but he felt a glow of excitement. "Is that so? Who was he?"

"Mr. Smith. A tall, well set-up gentleman, dark hair."

"Face like a fish?"

"That's him."

"Thankee kindly." Gaviston! His short legs moved like well-oiled pistons as he hastened back to the carriage, only to find it had left without him. He headed down the street, muttering under his breath.

In the small gray brick house, Madame returned to her client, a tall, well set-up gentleman with dark hair and a face like a fish. What was Lily up to, that all these smarts were looking for her? She'd ought to send Lily a note warning her.

Chapter Twenty-five

Knowing that Gaviston was on Lily McGee's trail, Coffen knew he had already wasted too much time. He directed the new hackney driver to take him to 10 Mercer Street. Lily had come up in the world. The address was a respectable block of flats. He went in at the front door and read the nameplates. There it was: Miss McGee, 304. He began the ascent to the top floor, looking for any sign of either Lily or Gaviston. He tiptoed down an uncarpeted corridor to number 304, tapped once, twice, a third time. No answer. He hoped that Lily had gotten away safely, but supposing she was in there, bleeding to death.

He tried the door, and to his surprise, it opened. The door led straight into the parlor. The light from the hall showed him a small, genteel room. The sofa and one upholstered chair were newish; the tables and occasional pieces were antiques. Probably Robinson's handiwork. The place was as tidy as could be, which suggested that Lily had left on her own.

He found a tinderbox and lit a lamp to look into the other rooms. The kitchen was as neat as a ball of wax. No body under the table or behind the stove. There was a cubbyhole off the kitchen, it looked like a servant's room—empty. The only other room was the bedroom. It, too, was undisturbed. The canopied bed with garish scarlet hangings, the clothespress and toilet table pretty well filled up the small room. The clothespress held only a few items of winter apparel. Lily had made good her escape, then. He looked under the bed, the only place large enough to conceal a body. He found nothing but a few dust balls.

Immensely relieved, Coffen left the flat and went back down to the hackney, which was waiting for him this time. Night had fallen and no two ways about it. The sky had darkened from navy blue to jet-black, with a big moon and a fistful of stars blinking down at him. "Brook's," he called to the driver, as he hopped into the hackney.

A few heads turned to see a blue jacket and fawn trousers enter the prestigious Brook's Club after 8:00 P.M. When Coffen went into the dining room, he found Prance and Luten already at the table, also in their afternoon jackets.

"What kept you?" Prance demanded. "You stopped to eat dinner, Pattle. Don't bother to deny it. And who shall blame you? They serve nothing here but the eternal beefsteak or joint with a boiled fowl and oyster sauce. We ordered you the joint."

"Thankee, for I've not eaten a bite." He pulled out his chair, poured a glass of wine, and assumed an important face for his disclosure.

"You've found her!" Prance exclaimed.

Coffen scowled to have his thunder stolen in this abrupt manner. "Nothing of the sort," he said. "She ain't there."

"Ain't where?" Prance demanded.

"At her flat on Mercer Street, third floor, or at Madame Labarre's either. She left there some time ago. And Gaviston knows it."

The arrival of his joint delayed an avalanche of questions from his companions. "Tewksbury mustard," he said, looking around the table. Prance passed the mustard. "And a dab of that horseradish." Luten passed the horseradish.

"Get on with it, Pattle!" Luten said, as soon as the waiter had left. "How does Gaviston know? Did you see him?"

"No, but Labarre said he'd been there, asking for Lily's address."

"He was where? And who the hell is Lily?"

"And from whence comes Madame Labarre?" Prance added in confusion.

"Robinson's redhead is Lily McGee, and Labarre is a witch. Gaviston was looking for Lily at the fortune teller's."

"He's lost whatever bit of brains he ever had," Prance murmured to Luten.

"No," Luten replied. "He's onto something. If we could only pry it out of him." He snatched Coffen's fork. "Just tell us the whole thing from the beginning, Pattle."

Coffen told the story, with many interruptions for clarification and eating. Prance insisted he have his fork back. He refused to watch a grown man eat mashed potatoes with his fingers.

When the tale had been told, Luten said, "Good work, Pattle. You should be knighted."

"He's already benighted," Prance murmured. "But this is no time for punning. You have outdone yourself, Coffen. You're a regular game dog."

"All in a day's work," Coffen said modestly, and poured them all a glass of wine, accidentally splashing it all over Prance.

"Have a care! I'm not waterproof!" Prance grouched, brushing at his blue superfine.

Luten said, "I expect Gaviston feels safe for the time being, with Lily gone. He might be home by now. We still want Baxter to identify him."

"Where do we do it?" Prance asked. He lifted the skin from the boiled fowl with his fork and frowned at it. "Not at his home, in front of his mama. That would be too cruel. We shall have to lure him out somewhere."

Luten said, "I'll call on Gaviston and ask him to accompany me to the House for an emergency meeting."

"I'll have some apple tart before we go," Coffen said.

"It won't take him a minute. He devours food like a hungry hound," Prance said. "And really, you know, he's earned it. It is Coffen who has carried the day."

"A good-sized wedge of cheddar, mind," Coffen said to the waiter. "Apple tart without cheese is like a kiss without a sneeze."

Prance grimaced. "That's squeeze, Pattle. Really, you do invent the most disgusting images. I shall never eat apple tart again."

The apple tart and cheese were soon devoured. Luten drew the line at coffee. "We're going now," he said. *"Now!"*

"I do like to finish off with a nice cup of coffee," Coffen muttered as they herded him out.

They drove straight to Grosvenor Square. Luten went to the door, leaving the others in the carriage.

"What rough behavior this escapade has led us into," Prance said, looking at Luten's departing back. "What will Lady deCoventry think to see Luten paying an evening call in a blue jacket?"

Luten was gone less than a minute. He came out alone, scowling. "He hasn't been there all day. Where the hell can he be?" he said, as he climbed in.

"Might he have discovered where Lily was going, and gone after her?" Prance asked.

"I didn't see any address book at Lily's place," Coffen said. "She wouldn't have left it behind, or a forwarding address with the landlord, considering why she was shearing off."

Luten felt a sudden tightening in his chest. "She might have been in touch with Corinne," he said. "She tried to warn her before, but was interrupted. And Gaviston knew it. He might have gone after them both."

"Harry is now officially out of it, is he?" Prance enquired.

Luten glared at him and called to his coachman, "Berkeley Square, and don't spare the horses."

Luten's first alarm, when he reached Corinne's house, was to find a footman answering the door. "Where's Black?" he demanded.

"He went out with her ladyship, sir," the footman said.

The tightening in Luten's chest began to vibrate from the beating of his heart. He felt a dizziness, almost a faintness. "When?" he barked.

"Not ten minutes ago."

"Where to?"

"He didn't say—but he was driving a hackney coach."

"You mean they were driving *in* one."

"No, your lordship, he was driving it hisself. Mrs. Ballard had her ladyship's carriage. It was very strange. He told me nothing, except that I was to answer the door."

The blood began pounding in Luten's ears. The tightness in his chest left him short of breath. If anything happened to her! And the last words he had said to her were "Go to hell!"

"Gaviston's got her!" Coffen said in a voice of doom.

"Oh really, Coffen," Prance said. "Leave the dramatics to me. There is no reason to suppose . . . although it is odd," he said, looking uncertainly to Luten.

"Nothing odd about it," Coffen said. "We're assuming Gaviston knows Corinne was in touch with Lily McGee. He was looking for Lily. If he didn't find her at home, then he might think Lily had whiddled the whole scrap to Corinne. He'd have to silence them both. He's come up with some excuse to lure Corinne into his clutches."

"Oh Lord, I wish you would stop being right, Coffen," Prance said in a frightened whisper.

Luten fought down the rising panic that was so strong it made him feel nauseated. He had to keep all his wits about him now. She'd only been gone ten minutes. The bastard wouldn't have killed her yet. And Black was with her. Thank God for Black! A good man in a

200

pinch. The question was, where had she gone? And why had she gone? What lure could Gaviston have held out to ensure her compliance? She hadn't quite trusted the message, or why had she had Black masquerade as a coach driver?

The answer came to him as he stood with his heart slowing to a dull thud. Gaviston had told her Lily McGee wanted to meet her. Where? Where, where, *where*?

He felt a pressure on his arm and turned to see Coffen looking at him oddly. "She must have had a message, eh?" He turned to the footman.

"Only the note from his lordship," the footman said. "Black mentioned it."

"I didn't send her a message!" Luten said. "How could she have been duped a second time by the same old trick? Do you have the message?"

There was a frantic, futile search for it. The note was not there.

Prance said, "The rendezvous will be in some private, isolated spot."

"Hyde Park again?" Coffen suggested.

"Corinne would balk at that, I think," Prance said. "He might have set up the meeting at Robinson's shop. He's used it before. He knows it's unoccupied."

"Or Lily McGee's flat," Luten said. "If Gaviston spoke to the fortune teller, he knows that address. He knows Lily is gone, the flat standing idle. It's the likeliest place for Lily to choose. We'll split up. I'll go to Lily's place. What was that address again, Coffen?"

"Ten Mercer Street, flat three-oh-four. Are you sure you're up to it?" Coffen asked. "You're pale as death, Luten."

"I'm up to it," Luten said grimly.

"Right. I'm for Hyde Park," Coffen said.

"I'll try Robinson's," Prance added.

"Be sure you both take a pistol," Luten said, already heading out the door.

The others darted off to call their carriages, and pick

up their pistols. Luten leapt onto the driver's box and took the reins from his coachman. The whip cracked, and the horses bolted forward.

Chapter Twenty-six

"Gaviston!" Corinne said again. "What are you doing here? Is Luten here?"

"I had a note from him," he replied. "He asked me to come. He's waiting for us in Miss McGee's flat upstairs." He wanted to use Lily's flat. Lily would think twice about making trouble when she read of the body being found in her own parlor.

"Is Miss McGee Robinson's friend?"

"That's right." He frowned. "Didn't you know?"

"I didn't know her name. Oh dear! Was it Harry after all?" She couldn't imagine why else Luten would have asked Gaviston along.

"I'm afraid so," he said, rushing her up the staircase. So Harry was the suspect! Idiots! As if Harry had the wits to engineer this job. If he'd known they suspected Harry, he needn't have bothered hiring those French thugs to hold up Corinne's carriage, nor sent that one genuine pearl, wrapped in French newsprint. At the time, it had seemed a good notion to point a finger at the Frenchies. Corinne obviously suspected them. Rose must have been boasting of having attached Monsieur de Carteret, his *nom de guerre* when he was seeing her.

"I can hardly believe it," Corinne said.

"I've seen it coming," he said sadly. "The gambling . . . I've tried to straighten him out."

"Do your parents know?"

"Not yet." They reached the second landing. "Of course Papa won't say anything about Harry's stealing the pearls, but for the rest, I don't know how it might be swept under the carpet. That's what Luten wants to discuss."

It seemed strange that Luten would connive at protecting Harry. That had certainly not been his intention earlier. In fact, she found it hard to believe Harry was guilty. "Why did Baxter not recognize Harry?" she asked.

Gaviston turned, a question in his eyes. "Baxter?"

"The man who looks after the flats where Rose Grimm lived. He said it wasn't Harry who called on her."

"Oh. Where did he get a look at Harry?"

"Didn't Luten tell you?"

"I haven't spoken to him. I had a note asking me to come."

"It was at Covent Garden." They reached the top landing and turned left.

"So that's why you invited Harry." Corinne noticed the angry edge to his words, but could hardly blame him. She had disliked doing it herself. "Here is Rose's flat, number three-oh-four," he said, opening the door.

The minute she stepped inside, she realized Luten wasn't there, or the redheaded woman either. Gaviston turned the key in the lock, removed it and put it in his pocket. It was just her and Gaviston, locked in the flat, with Gaviston blocking her way to the door. The coziness of the little parlor only added to the sense of menace. Gaviston no longer bothered to hide his intentions. His face was set in hard lines of hatred. Her mind darted over the events leading to this situation.

The note from Luten was another forgery, then, written to lure her, alone, to this isolated spot. Why had he brought her here? There could be only one reason. He was going to kill her. So it was Gaviston who had written Robinson that forged letter asking him to steal the pearls, and killed him and Rose Grimm.

She stood perfectly silent, staring into his eyes as if

mesmerized. "Why did you do it?" she asked in a hollow voice.

"It's all your fault! That necklace belonged to me by rights! I didn't know the court was going to make you give it back. Then when Papa decided to have it insured, I knew it would come to light that the pearls were false."

"So it was a forgery!"

"Of course it was, and who but myself could have had such a good forgery made? That technique is only perfected in Austria. The pearls didn't belong to you! You got more than you deserved! A common Irish bog trotter, lording it over us, hoodwinking that old fool of a George into believing that you loved him, stealing my inheritance. You're no better than a whore! A damned Irish whore! You're all alike, fleecing us of our hard-earned money."

His face contorted in rage as the hatred came spewing out, until she felt soiled just hearing it. He was not only going to kill her, he had convinced himself it was a duty, and he was going to enjoy it. She stood perfectly still while a tide of abuse washed over her. As she stood, she surreptitiously slid her hand into her pocket, felt the comforting outlines of the small pistol, and wrapped her fingers around the handle. But would she have the fortitude to use it? George had taught her how to shoot, but she had never shot a living creature in her life, not even a rabbit. She could only shoot Gaviston if he was aiming his pistol at her. Or did he mean to strangle her, as he had strangled Rose? He wasn't holding a gun.

Her throat was achingly dry, but her fingers on the gun were slick with perspiration. She wondered if Black would come back. Very likely he had mistaken Gaviston for Luten at the doorway, as she had. She was on her own. And Gaviston kept himself firmly planted between her and the door that led out. The locked door.

When he stopped for breath, she spoke. "How did you get hold of the pearls?" she asked, fingering the pistol butt, praying that Black would come.

"You shouldn't have taken the Kent dresser," he said, pleased with himself. "I knew George kept the key to his safe in that secret compartment. I got Harry drunk the night before I left for Austria. Called on him for a farewell drink, just the two of us. I took the pearls with me to Austria. I had a copy made and sold the original to Count Kaunitz, for his mistress—another whore—and substituted the fakes when I came back to London. You never knew the difference. But then what would a woman like you know about quality?"

So he hadn't used Gregory. Gregory must have been killed by Lefty Muldoon after all. As they talked, they watched each other like cat and mouse. Gaviston's first bout of fury had subsided to a determined calm that was even more frightening.

"But we're wasting time, Countess. I am due at a rout party. Lady Angela will be unhappy if I'm late." As he spoke, he pulled a length of white cord from his pocket and stretched it between his hands.

Her heart pounded so hard she could feel it pulse in her throat, in her head, even her fingertips. Her breath came in shallow gasps.

"Don't bother to shout," he said, in a voice of silken menace. "This is a corner flat. The one next door is empty. It won't hurt much. Rose died in a minute."

If only Black would come! She must try to keep him talking, to delay the inevitable, but it was hard to speak for the dryness in her throat. "Why did you use Rose? Why didn't you just have Robinson buy a costume?" she asked.

"I had no intention of using Rose, originally. She was just a convenience after I broke with my mistress. The simpleton actually offered to borrow a costume for me, hoping I'd take her with me to the masquerade. As if I'd be seen in public with the likes of her. When she mentioned the Robin Hood outfit, I remembered Luten's ball, and thought it might make Robinson's job easier if you mistook him for Luten. Robinson was about his size. It was my only mistake, not telling Robinson to make sure he gave me back the costume. He was to have dinner with his whore, and left the costume behind. I realized when Rose told me you were enquiring at Drury Lane that she couldn't be counted on to hold her tongue if you turned Bow Street on her. The lower classes are unreliable.

"I had no intention of killing Robinson—not that he's any loss to society. It was his own fault for leaving the costume behind and setting you and Luten on his trail. I knew that damned bulldog of a Luten would hound me down sooner or later. All I wanted was the pearls. I never planned to kill anyone."

"Why did you want to involve Luten? He's never done you any harm."

"No harm? No *harm*? The man's an anarchist, wanting to give power to the lower orders. You know what happened in France when the rabble took over. They're not fit to rule themselves, and he's not fit to sit in Parliament. If it weren't for him, you'd be married to Harry by now, as you should be."

He came a step closer, stretching the white cord taut between his fingers. "But enough chatter. The time has come, Countess."

He made a lunge at her. She stepped back, drawing out the pistol and aiming it at him. He froze momentarily, trying to decide whether she'd really use it.

"I'll shoot if I have to, Gaviston," she said, in a frightened voice. "Unlock the door. Let me go, and I won't shoot you."

He held his hands up, dropping the cord and holding her gaze. "You win," he said. Even as he uttered the words, his right foot came up and kicked the pistol out of her hand. It clattered under the sofa. Corinne threw herself to the floor, reaching for it. Gaviston was on top of her, his hand pushing hers aside. She felt the tip of the handle—but if she drew it out, he'd take it from her before she could aim and shoot. She drew out her empty hand.

Gaviston stood up and pulled her up after him.

"Bitch!" he growled, and lifting his hand, he struck her a blow across the cheek with all a grown man's force. She fell, reeling against the sofa, and slid to the floor. Gaviston was on top of her, his fingers around her throat, while she kicked and flailed her arms and whimpered. And all the time his fingers tightened harder, harder, squeezing the life out of her.

Chapter Twenty-seven

"Ten Mercer Street," the coachman said. "That's it, milord."

Luten drew the team to a stop, flung the ribbons to the coachman and leapt down from the box. As he headed to the house, another coach driver appeared from the shadows and came running up to him. "Your lordship!" the man exclaimed.

"Black?"

"It's me. But you—I thought it was you that took her ladyship into that house," Black said, looking to number ten.

"She's gone in there alone?"

"She thought it was you! Your note said to meet her and the redheaded woman in there."

"How long ago?"

"Not long. I've been up and down the block twice."

Luten bounded into the building, up the stairs, with Black a step behind him. He ran down the hall, glancing at the door numbers. When he got to 304, he turned the knob and found it locked. But he knew she was in there. He heard sounds of a scuffle.

"Gaviston!" he bellowed. "You son of a bitch, if you hurt her, I'll kill you." The sound of cracking wood overrode his words as he lifted a booted foot and kicked in the door.

No one was to be seen in the little parlor, but he heard a stifled whimpering. Thank God she was alive! He charged in, looking all around, and saw them on the floor in front of the sofa, with Gaviston on top of Corinne, his hand clamped over her mouth to prevent her from shouting. Gaviston's head turned as Luten drew out his pistol. There was a quiet, ominous click as he released the safety catch.

Corinne pushed Gaviston aside and sat up, clutching her throat and gasping. When she had caught her breath she rasped, "He doesn't have a gun!" She retrieved her own gun from beneath the sofa. Black took it and helped her up. Her hair was all askew and her bonnet was hanging down her back by its ribbons.

"Oh Luten, he was going to strangle me,"she said, and pitched herself into his arms, which closed protectively around her. Her body was racked with dry, wrenching sobs as she clung to him, and he held her with a fierce tenderness.

Black pointed Corinne's pistol at Gaviston. "Up on your feet, mister," he said.

"That's *Lord* Gaviston," Gaviston said, and rose stiffly, brushing off his jacket.

"It's all right, Corinne," Luten said. "It's all right, my dear. It's over now." But he knew it wouldn't be all over for either of them for a long time. She would have nightmares of this ordeal, and the vision of her wild eyes staring up from the floor would haunt his dreams for many a night to come. When she had stopped trembling, he said, "Go home with Black. You'll be safe there. I'll take care of Gaviston."

"He admitted everything," she said.

Corinne averted her head as Black led Gaviston down the stairs. She couldn't bear to look at him. When Luten tried to lead her down behind them, her knees collapsed. She was too faint to walk. He swept her into his arms and carried her down, gently, as if she might break. Neither of them spoke, but it was a speaking sort of silence. When he placed her in his coach, he gazed at her a moment. "It's all over, love," he said.

She just nodded, and smiled a travesty of a smile.

Black drove her home in Luten's carriage. She sat huddled in the corner, with her arms wrapped around her for warmth. Luten's coachman drove the hired rig to Bow Street, with Luten and Gaviston inside. Neither of them spoke until they reached Bow Street.

On Berkeley Square, Black enjoyed a few more moments of glory, ordering servants about to bring her ladyship a glass of brandy and a blanket, and sitting with her on her sofa, comforting her. When she was sufficiently recovered to go abovestairs, he personally accompanied her up to her chamber, from which point Lord Blackwell's courtship continued only in his head.

By the time Luten returned, Corinne had tidied her hair and put on a chiffon scarf to conceal the bruises at her throat, but her face was still white, and her dilated pupils made her eyes look like two glittering black gems. Prance and Coffen had not returned yet. She sat alone by the grate, brooding. She put out her hand to draw Luten down beside her. When he sat down, she held on to his fingers tightly. The night was cool, and Black had lit a fire to ease her trembling.

Luten gazed at the play of light and shadows on her lovely face. He wished he could marry her that very night, take her home with him to make sure nothing like this ever happened to her again. He drew her into his arms and kissed her once, lightly, just to assure himself he wasn't dreaming.

She placed her fevered hands on his cheeks and said in a wan voice, "How did you know where to find me?"

"We've had a busy day," he said, and outlined what he and the others had been doing.

"I was a fool to believe a forged note a second time, but I couldn't miss a chance to talk to the redheaded woman. We'll have to find her for the trial."

"There won't be any trial. Gaviston's dead, shot himself. He asked me to let him take the gentleman's way out. I gave him the opportunity, as the alternative was certain hanging. I left a pistol with one bullet in it on the

211

floor of the carriage when I got out. I made him write and sign a confession first, of course."

"I daresay it's for the best. It will avoid the shame and scandal of a public trial. DeCoventry won't give me any trouble about the pearls now."

"He knows the whole story. Townsend went to call on him. It wasn't concern for the equivocal position Gaviston had put you in that made him write his confession. He did it for the family. Gaviston didn't want any suspicions to besmirch the family escutcheon. *Noblesse oblige*, was the phrase he used. The family title meant so much to him. Too much. He's found his place on the family tree as one of the black sheep. Such an unlikely black sheep, considering his pose as the good son."

"And the pearls have ended up with some lightskirt in Austria," Corinne said.

"I expect he would have let the forgery be discovered and blamed you if he'd known about Gregory. He thought the fakes could only be made in Austria, and as that pointed to him, he had to be rid of them. Our wasted day at Maidstone was to give him time to hunt for Lily McGee. The one pearl he sent to you is from the original necklace. He removed it to serve as a model for the forger in Austria and never put it back on the necklace."

Corinne set down her glass and turned to him. "I'll send it to Lady deCoventry. I don't want any reminder of that necklace. How can I ever thank you, Luten?"

He seized her two hands. "By forgiving me for telling you to go to hell. That has sat like a lead weight on my heart through all this wretched, interminable day."

"I knew you didn't mean it."

"I was just jealous as a green cow of Harry."

"I told you, he's like a brother to me. Were you really jealous?" she asked, pleased.

"I can't think why else I kept suspecting him after Baxter exonerated him completely." His hands began moving up her arms toward her shoulders. "You mentioned wanting to thank me. I believe the hero is usually rewarded by—" He hesitated. Should he come right out with the proposal, while she was in a gracious mood?

"By a kiss," she said, and leaned forward to place a light buss on his cheek.

"I don't call that a kiss, Countess," he said, and pulled her into his arms for a more satisfactory reward.

A warm and languorous glow seeped through Corinne as they sat, locked in embrace, with the lights and shadows from the fire flickering over them.

When he released her, he said, "I've been wanting to do that ever since the first time I saw you walk into Almack's on George's arm, looking lost and frightened, and so beautiful my teeth ached."

"Was it a toothache that put that scowl on your face?"

"You remember our first meeting, too! I take that as a hopeful sign. No, it was the fact that you were George's wife, when every fiber of my body told me you should be mine."

"But you went to Appleby to offer for Susan after George was dead."

"My devious brain was using Susan as an excuse to go after you. Darling, I—"

He was interrupted by a rap at the front door, followed by Black's rushing footsteps. Prance and Coffen came pelting in.

"What is this?" Prance demanded. "You've been here, cozy as a pair of mice in malt while I lurked like a stray dog outside Robinson's shop, fighting off two mangy curs and assorted obscene offers which I shan't detail in front of a lady!"

"How about me?" Coffen scowled. "That park was as eerie as a graveyard. There's owls there, a whole flock of them."

"A parliament, Coffen," Prance said.

"Eh? You're mad. Parliament don't meet in Hyde Park."

"A flock of starlings, a gaggle of geese and a parliament of owls. That is the proper terminology. Some quite

213

misplaced reference to the wisdom of the owl and the honorable members, perhaps."

"Anyhow, there was a whole flock of 'em hooting their heads off," Coffen said.

"You're incorrigible," Prance declared, lifting his coattails and perching on the edge of a chair. "One might as well speak to the walls." Then he turned to the others. "Well, what happened? I am vastly relieved to see Corinne got home safe and sound, *ça va sans dire.*"

Luten began to outline the sorry tale.

"Before you get into it, could we have a bit to eat?" Coffen said. "And coffee. I missed my coffee at dinner. If you can call bolting a mouthful of beef dinner."

"You are forgetting the apple tart and cheddar," Prance said.

"Thankee for reminding me. I'd like some apple tart as well if you have any, Corinne."

"I'll speak to Black," she said, and rose reluctantly from the sofa to go after him.

Prance said archly, "Do I smell April and May, Luten?"

"It's likely me you're whiffing," Coffen said. "I fell into some nice-smelling bushes at the park. White blossoms."

"You smell April," Luten said. "I don't have confirmation on May."

"She hasn't said yes, then?" Prance asked, eyes dancing.

"She hasn't said no. As soon as Coffen has had his coffee, you two shab off. Understood?"

"Compris," Prance said, "and *bonne chance*, Luten. I daresay etiquette demands that I wish you well, though I shall be praying for a refusal."

"I ain't stirring one inch until I've had my apple tart," Coffen asserted, and took up possession of the seat vacated by Corinne. "This is cozy. I like a fire."

"Shall I chuck him into it?" Prance asked Luten.

"Better not. A fat fire is a dangerous thing."

"Let Coffen have his tart. We owe a good deal to him. If it hadn't been for him . . ."

Prance shivered and moved close to the blaze. "Don't say it, Luten, I pray. To think of Corinne with her face blue or a bullet in her velvet bosom has quite undone me."

"Shut up, Prance," Coffen said. "You'll be putting me off my feed with that kind of talk. Tahrsome fellow."

Corinne returned, followed by Black with the coffee and apple tart and a few other dainties, and they pieced together the story, surmising when they were unsure of the facts.

"I never liked Gaviston, but I never imagined he was actually evil," Corinne said.

"Perhaps just mad," Prance said, carving up an olive with his knife and fork. "In any case, the man is dead. *Nil nisi bonum.*" He set aside his plate, glanced at the French clock on the mantel, and rose. "It's time we let this little lady get some rest."

There was a general commotion of rising and leave-taking and talk of meeting on the morrow. Luten remained behind. He closed the saloon door, then stalked toward Corinne in a determined manner. "If anyone else comes through that door—"

As he spoke, there was a discreet tap at the door. "I'm back from my card game, milady," Mrs. Ballard called in a questioning voice. "Can I get you anything before I retire?"

"No," Luten called back.

The echo of a whispered colloquy between Mrs. Ballard and Black was heard. "Are you all right, my dear?" Mrs. Ballard asked.

"Get rid of her," Luten said under his breath.

"I'm fine, Mrs. Ballard," Corinne said. "You can go to bed. I shall be up shortly."

"No trouble to wait for you, dear."

"Go away!" Luten shouted.

"Luten!" Corinne exclaimed. "You're acting very high in the instep! This is my house."

"You need a firm hand."

"Just because you rescued me tonight—"

"Saved your life!"

"That doesn't give you the right to order my servants about in my house."

"Well if that's your idea of gratitude!"

"I said thank you. Thank you very much," she said crossly. "I am extremely obliged to you."

"Go to hell!" Luten said. He threw open the door, shoved Black aside and took two steps into the hallway. Then he returned, wearing a sheepish expression. "I expect you'll want to sleep in tomorrow. I shall be in touch with you, not too early."

"Thank you, dear Luten," she said with a fond smile. "I look forward to your—touch."

Luten's frown had dwindled to a half-smile as he darted across the street. Prance, watching from his saloon window, uttered a high, disbelieving laugh. How could Luten possibly have failed, when all was so patently in his favor? Should he nip out and enquire? No, let it wait until tomorrow. He would have thought up something clever to say by then. He would just ask André to draw him a hot bath to soak away the stench of Shepherd's Market, followed by a posset, with a soupçon of brandy to lull him into the arms of Morpheus. To sleep, perchance to dream . . .

Love Letters

Ballantine romances are on the Web!

Read about your favorite Ballantine authors and upcoming books on our Web site, LOVE LETTERS, at **www.randomhouse.com/BB/loveletters**, including:

♥What's new in the stores
♥Previews of upcoming books
♥In-depth interviews with romance authors and publishing insiders
♥Sample chapters from new romances
♥And more . . .

Want to keep in touch? To subscribe to Love Notes, the monthly what's-new update for the Love Letters Web site, send an e-mail message to **loveletters@cruises.randomhouse.com** with "subscribe" as the subject of the message. You will receive a monthly announcement of the latest news and features on our site.

So follow your heart and visit us at **www.randomhouse.com/BB/loveletters**!

*Lorrie Morgan was born to be
a country-western music star.*

In FOREVER YOURS FAITHFULLY,
she tells us her tempestuous story of sweet
triumph and bitter tragedy.
From her childhood as a Nashville blueblood
performing at the Grand Ole Opry at the tender
age of eleven to her turbulent,
star-crossed love affair with Keith Whitley,
a bluegrass legend she loved passionately
but could not save from his personal demons,
to her rise to superstardom,
she lays bare all the secrets and great passions
of a life lived to the fullest.

And her story would not be complete without
the music that has been her lifeline.

**A special four-song CD of
never-before-released material,
featuring a duet with Keith Whitley,
is included with this hardcover.**

FOREVER YOURS FAITHFULLY
by Lorrie Morgan

Published by Ballantine Books.
Coming to bookstores everywhere
in October 1997.

Diana Palmer's
sizzling historical novels are full of soul-stirring
emotion and rich storytelling. Now she carries on her
bestselling tradition with

THE SAVAGE HEART

the fiery story of a woman with big dreams and a man
who has nothing to believe in . . . except her.

Lethal to foes and generous to friends, the enigmatic
Matt Davis can handle anything that comes his way
until Tess Meredith storms into Chicago and back into
his life. And this fearless and determined young cru-
sader is ready to wage her greatest battle . . . for a love
that will not be denied.

THE SAVAGE HEART comes to you in a brand-new
format as a lightweight, durable, elegant, affordably
priced (only $10) petite hardcover.

On sale September 2 at bookstores everywhere.

*Read on for more titles also available in this thrilling new
format from Fawcett Columbine . . .*